David James

Series Editor: Marian C

Birdsong

Sebastian Faulks

Philip Allan Updates, an imprint of Hodder Education, part of Hachette UK, Market Place, Deddington, Oxfordshire OX15 0SE

Orders
Bookpoint Ltd, 130 Milton Park, Abingdon, Oxfordshire, OX14 4SB
tel: 01235 827720
fax: 01235 400454
e-mail: uk.orders@bookpoint.co.uk
Lines are open 9.00 a.m.–5.00 p.m., Monday to Saturday, with a 24-hour message answering service. You can also order through the Philip Allan Updates website: www.philipallan.co.uk

ISBN 978-0-340-96574-0

First printed 2009

Impression number 5 4 3 2 1

Year 2014 2013 2012 2011 2010 2009

Printed in Malta

Environmental information
Hachette UK's policy is to use papers that are natural, renewable and recyclable products and made from wood grown in sustainable forests. The logging and manufacturing processes are expected to conform to the environmental regulations of the country of origin.

Contents

Introduction

Aims of the guide

The purpose of this Student Text Guide to Sebastian Faulks's best-selling novel *Birdsong* is to enable you to organise your thoughts and responses to the novel, to deepen your understanding of key features and aspects, and to help you to address the particular requirements of examination questions in order to obtain the best possible grade. It will also prove useful to those writing a coursework piece on the novel by providing summaries, lists, analyses and references to help with the content and construction of the assignment.

It is assumed that you have read and studied the novel already under the guidance of a teacher or lecturer. This is a revision guide, not an introduction, although some of its content serves the purpose of providing initial background. It can be read in its entirety, or it can be dipped into and used as a reference guide to specific and separate aspects of the novel.

The remainder of this Introduction consists of Assessment Objectives, which summarise the requirements of the schemes of assessment employed by the various exam boards and revision advice, which gives a suggested programme for using the material in the guide.

The Text Guidance section consists of a series of subsections that examine key aspects of the book including contexts, chapter summaries and commentary, characters, themes and language. Terms defined in 'Literary terms and concepts' on pp. 78–80 are highlighted the first time they appear in this section.

The final section, Questions and Answers, gives brief practical advice on writing essay answers of various types, along with mark schemes, model essay plans and some examples of marked work.

Assessment Objectives

The AOs for A-level English Literature from 2008 are common to all boards:

AO1	articulate creative, informed and relevant responses to literary texts, using appropriate terminology and concepts, and coherent, accurate written expression
AO2	demonstrate detailed critical understanding in analysing the ways in which structure, form and language shape meanings in literary texts
AO3	explore connections and comparisons between different literary texts, informed by interpretations of other readers
AO4	demonstrate understanding of the significance and influence of the contexts in which literary texts are written and received

Revision advice

For the examined units it is possible that either brief or extensive revision will be necessary because the original study of the text took place some time previously. It is therefore useful to know how to approach revision and which tried and tested methods are considered the most successful.

Don't:

- leave it until the last minute
- assume you remember the text well enough and don't need to revise at all
- spend hours designing a beautiful revision schedule
- revise more than one text at the same time
- think you don't need to revise because it is an open-book exam
- decide in advance what you think the questions will be and revise only for those
- try to memorise particular essay plans
- reread texts randomly and aimlessly
- revise for longer than two hours in one sitting
- miss school lessons in order to work alone at home
- try to learn a whole ring-binder's worth of work
- tell yourself that character and plot revision is enough
- imagine that watching the video again is the best way to revise
- rely on a study guide instead of the text

There are no short cuts to effective exam revision; the only way to know a text well, and to know your way around it in an exam, is to have done the necessary studying. If you use the following six-stage method you will not only manage to revisit and reassess all previous work on the text but will be able to distil, organise and retain your knowledge.

(1) Between a month and a fortnight before the exam, depending on your schedule (which should be a simple list of stages with dates), you will need to read the text again, this time taking stock of all the underlinings and marginal annotations as well. As you read, collect onto sheets of A4 the essential ideas and quotations. The acts of selecting key material and recording it as notes are natural ways of stimulating thought and aiding memory.

(2) Reread the highlighted areas and marginal annotations in your critical extracts and background handouts, and add anything useful from them to your list of notes and quotations. Then read your previous essays and the teacher's comments again. As you look back through essays written earlier in the course you should have the pleasant sensation of realising that you are now able to write much better essays than you could before. You will also discover that much of your huge file of notes is

redundant or repeated, and that you have changed your mind about some beliefs, so the distillation process is not too daunting. Selecting what is important is the way to crystallise your knowledge and understanding.

(3) During the run-up to the exam you need to make lots of practice essay plans to help you identify any gaps in your knowledge and give you practice in planning in five to eight minutes. Past-paper titles for you to plan are provided in this guide, some of which can be done as full timed essays — and marked strictly according to exam criteria — which will show whether length and timing are problematic for you. If you have not seen a copy of a real exam paper before you take your first module, ask to see a past paper so that you are familiar with the layout, rubric and types of question. For each text you are studying for the examination you need to know exactly which Assessment Objectives are being tested and where the heaviest weighting falls, as well as whether it is a closed or open-book exam. It would also be helpful if your teacher shared with you the examiners' reports on past papers.

(4) About a week before the exam, reduce your two or three sides of A4 notes to the size of a double-sided postcard of small, dense writing. Collect a group of key words by once again selecting and condensing, using abbreviations for quotations (first and last word), and character and place names (initials). Choosing and writing out the short quotations will help you to focus on the essential issues, and to recall them quickly in the exam. Make sure that your selection covers the main themes and includes examples of imagery, language, style, comments on character, examples of irony and other significant aspects of the text. Previous class discussion and essay writing will have indicated which quotations are useful for almost any essay title; select those that can serve more than one purpose. In this way a minimum number of quotations can have maximum application.

(5) You now have in a compact, accessible form all the material for any possible essay title. There are only half a dozen themes relevant to a literary text — though be aware that they may be expressed in a variety of ways — so if you have covered these you should not meet with any nasty surprises when you read the exam questions. You don't need to refer to your file of paperwork again, or even to the text. For the few days before the exam you can read through your handy postcard whenever and wherever you get the opportunity. Each time you read it, which will only take a few minutes, you are reminding yourself of all the information you will be able to recall in the exam to adapt to the general title or to support an analysis of particular passages.

(6) A fresh, active mind works wonders, and information needs time to settle, so don't try to cram just before the exam. Get a good night's sleep the night before so that you will be able to enter the exam room feeling the confidence of the well-prepared but relaxed candidate.

Text Guidance

Contexts

Life and works of Sebastian Faulks

Sebastian Faulks was born on 20 April 1953. His father was a judge and diplomat, his mother an actress. He attended Wellington College and Emmanuel College, Cambridge. After a short spell as a teacher he became a journalist: he worked on the *Daily Telegraph*, the *Sunday Telegraph* and in 1986 became literary editor for the *Independent on Sunday*. After rising to become deputy editor of that newspaper he left, partly in protest over staff cuts, but also to concentrate on his career as a writer. He continues to review books and write articles for numerous newspapers and magazines both in this country and abroad.

His first novel, *A Trick of the Light*, was published in 1984 when he was 31, and it met with mixed reviews. *The Girl at the Lion d'Or*, published in 1989, fared better, and it also marked the beginning of his interest in France and the First World War, subject matters which would reach their apogee in his next (and most famous) novel, *Birdsong*, that was published in 1993. It established him as a first-rank novelist, gaining great critical and commercial success. The third book in this 'trilogy' (a term that can only be loosely applied to these three novels) was completed with the publication of *Charlotte Gray* in 1998. This novel was made into a moderately successful film in 2001. *On Green Dolphin Street* was published in 2001, followed by *Human Traces* in 2005. His latest novel, *Engleby*, published in 2007, received good reviews and marks a new departure for Faulks, being a novel set in England about a man who bears a striking resemblance to the author himself.

In 2008 he published *Devil May Care*, an officially endorsed James Bond novel. Unusually, Faulks was billed on the cover as 'writing as Ian Fleming', and he described it as close to Fleming's **style**, without being **pastiche**. The book was well received critically and became the fastest-selling hardback in Penguin's history.

Faulks will always divide critics: novelists who engage with complex ideas, and who refuse to be confined or defined by reviewers, have traditionally in the UK attracted hostile criticism from the quality press and the literary journals and magazines. Faulks has now achieved the level of success (which was confirmed with the award of the CBE in 2002) that means his core readers (of whom there are many) will continue to buy his books knowing full well that although he might baffle them, he will delight and surprise them as well. He remains one of the most original and challenging authors writing in English today.

The modern age

For many historians and literary critics, the modern age began in 1914 with the outbreak of the Great War (for obvious reasons it was only known as the First World War after the Second World War had broken out). On reflection, this date signalled the end of many things: the class system was ruptured, the political classes were challenged, the military was almost completely destroyed, and some felt that inherited authority would no longer be able to rule unchallenged. Between the death of Queen Victoria (in 1901) and the declaration of war, Britain and much of Europe had enjoyed a *belle époque* (a beautiful era) — an optimistic time that produced great art, and when some enjoyed great privilege. The First World War fundamentally changed our view of history: as Geoff Dyer wrote in *The Missing of the Somme* (2001): '...the past *as past* was preserved by the war that shattered it. By ushering in a future characterised by instability and uncertainty, it embalmed for ever a past characterised by stability and certainty.'

George V

King George V was crowned in Westminster Abbey on 22 June 1911. He was a politically astute, if somewhat dull, man. It was he who, in 1917, and in order to appease British nationalist feelings, changed the royal family name of Saxe-Coburg-Gotha to Windsor. It was the king who advised his then prime minister, David Lloyd-George, not to offer asylum to his first cousin, Tsar Nicholas II of Russia and his family, when the Russian Revolution broke out in 1917. The Romanovs, George felt, might be an unsettling influence in the country. They were shot soon after by revolutionary guards. Such actions suggest a ruthlessness that, given the uncertainties of the time, possibly helped save the British monarchy when many others in Europe were swept away by the forces unleashed by the war.

A changing society

At the beginning of the twentieth century Britain was still governed by men who had inherited their wealth from the land. But not for much longer. Britain had undergone an industrial revolution in the nineteenth century that had transformed urban and rural areas; but this process of change did not slow down with a new monarch. The census taken in 1901 shows that over 25 million Britons lived in urban areas (4.5 million in London) and 7.5 million in the countryside. By 1911, 41% of the population of England and Wales lived in London and the industrialised areas of the North and the Midlands. Population shifts continued to alter the demographic make-up of the country: this was the age of mass emigration to North America and Australia (at the peak, in 1912, 268,485 people left British shores for new lives abroad). The population was ageing too, which made the loss of an entire generation even more catastrophic.

Class

No discussion of any period in the history of Great Britain would be complete without class at its centre. The country had undergone a period of rapid industrialisation in the nineteenth century, and this brought previously unimaginable riches, as well as extreme squalor and deprivation. It is tempting to view the Victorian period through the often graphic but subjective lens of Dickens's prose, but although the Victorian ruling class was responsible for enforcing working conditions which, to a modern eye, were astonishingly cruel, it was also capable of change. By the end of the nineteenth century compulsory education for children was on the statute books, slavery had been abolished, public lending libraries and parks were established, paid holidays accepted, public transport, in the form of trams, buses, the underground and the most extensive rail network in Europe, were all widely available, making the late nineteenth century a period of remarkable mobility — both physical or social. The momentum established at this time increased with the Edwardians.

Class, however, continued to underpin society at every level, as is evident in *Birdsong* throughout the passages set in the trenches. Jack Firebrace is the epitome of the decent, hard-working labourer who literally helped build the foundations of empire. The officer class is equally representative of the public school, Oxbridge-educated set of men who saw their power and status as a birthright. The First World War, among other things, forced these men to live and die side by side, and through this new intimacy it was obvious that the old divisions would have to be rearranged once peace had returned. It has been argued that the sense of duty that was so inculcated in the working man towards his social superiors made the sacrifices of the war more understandable; there were sporadic outbreaks of unrest in the British, French and German armies but, given the conditions and the number of deaths, it is remarkable that only one large-scale rebellion occurred. 'Never such innocence again,' said Larkin many years later, and he was right.

Work

Any society that undergoes such a rapid transformation is likely to see stark inequalities. The life of the average worker in Edwardian England was not a happy one. In 1911, 8.6% of the population of England and Wales lived two to a room, but in other areas the situation was far worse: in some parts of London it was 16.7%, and in the East End it was 36%. The author Jack London wrote in 1902:

> Nowhere in the streets of London may one escape the sight of abject poverty, while five minutes' walk from almost any point will bring one to a slum; but the region my hansom was now penetrating was one unending slum. The streets were filled with a new and different race of people, short of stature, and of wretched or beer-sodden appearance. We rolled along through miles of brick and squalor, and from each cross street and alley flashed long vistas of brick and misery.

Thousands were unemployed and homeless, the hated workhouses were still operating, offering squalid conditions and the smallest amount of food and drink in return for back-breaking work. This overcrowding was also prevalent in the expanding cities of the North and the Midlands.

Belle époque

But for many it was indeed a *belle époque*: this was an age of conspicuous consumption, a time when skilled workers, as well as Mr Pooter-like clerks and administrators, had more disposable income than they had ever had before. It was a time of a growing servant class, brought into being by the social aspirations of the new moneyed middle class. As they grew in affluence so they took flight from the crowded inner cities: they demanded new houses with gardens, away from the grime of the inner city, and it was this period that saw the growth of the suburbs. Those who wanted to shop in London could visit the new 'department store', Selfridges. Or they could pick up tips on how to furnish their newly acquired terraced suburban homes by visiting the *Daily Mail* Ideal Home Exhibition, established in 1908. This was an age of invention where one could look beyond the necessity for domestic staff and buy prototypes of the electric kettle, irons, washing machines and vacuum cleaners. A time was coming, it was hoped, when the machine would liberate people from the drudgery of labour, both at home and at work. The **irony** was that before that was to happen Europe would have to fight the first truly mechanised war. It was the age of the machine, but it would kill and maim just as much as it would liberate and transport.

World in motion

The first tanks were introduced in the First World War: they transformed the later stages of the conflict, particularly on the Western Front around Amiens in 1917, where they were used especially effectively to punch through the German defences (anything that could cut through the miles of murderous barbed wire would almost certainly bring the stalemate to an earlier end). This was the deadly culmination of a period that had seen a true revolution in transport: the tank was the logical end to human endeavour, born out of desperation.

The Edwardian era marked the dawn of an age obsessed with forms of transport that would transform the countryside and the city. The Victorians had laid the foundations of the most advanced railway system in the world (hence the **dramatic irony** of Bérard saying to Stephen: 'So there it is. They have trains now in England', which only serves to expose his ignorance), but the Edwardians added nearly 1,200 miles of track between 1900 and 1913. The age of the horse was in decline; but what replaced it was not any one, simple alternative form of transport, but many. The bicycle and the tricycle became common sights on the roads of Great Britain, with women in particular making great use of these cheap and fashionable alternatives to

the expensive and unpredictable horse. The 'motor vehicle', 'horseless carriage' or, more commonly, the car (an Americanism that soon replaced 'carriage') underwent huge changes before it became affordable for a sizeable proportion of the middle classes.

Planes, trains and automobiles

Those who could not afford to buy a car had the choice of ever-faster methods of transport to get to work, or to go on holiday. At the beginning of the twentieth century there was a profusion of different vehicles in London alone: one could travel by open-topped, horse-drawn omnibus, by motor bus, (horse-drawn) hansom carriage, motorised taxicab or by tram. The rapidly expanding Underground system (built by the many British and Irish Jack Firebraces) could deliver you quickly to your destination. Then there were the trains that brought in, and took out, the growing ranks of 'commuters'. The age that ended so savagely in 1914 was very much the 'golden age of steam': the railways opened up the country to hundreds of thousands of city dwellers who could use them because they were relatively cheap. Not surprisingly, class was integral even to this democratic method of transport, with the poorest members of society travelling third class, and the more affluent travelling first class.

The developments made on the ground were to some extent reflected in the sky. On 17 December 1903 the Wright brothers made history by successfully completing the first controlled, powered human flight in a machine that was heavier than air. The military took great interest in these developments, even funding certain projects. In 1912 the Royal Flying Corps was founded, which was to become, in 1918, the Royal Air Force. Progress, in both military and civilian terms, of this method of transport was swift; the first 'dog fights' between combatant aircraft took place in the First World War, as well as bombing raids on towns and cities. Aircraft, even more than the tank or the machine gun, would transform the nature of conflict and the tactics used by strategists.

Politics

Between 1902 and the outbreak of the First World War Britain had three prime ministers: these were (in order) Arthur Balfour (Conservative, PM from 1902–05), Sir Henry Campbell-Bannerman (Liberal, PM from 1905–08), and Herbert Asquith (Liberal, PM from 1908–16). Balfour and Asquith, although in many ways deeply conservative, began a process of constitutional change that would result in the Representation of the People Act of 1918. This abolished practically all property qualifications for men. Furthermore, for the first time it enfranchised women (but only those over 30 who met certain property qualifications). It was undeniably progress, but women were still not politically equal to men (who could vote from the age of 21); women did not gain full electoral equality for another ten years.

It was obvious that the two Houses of Parliament were over-represented by the landed gentry, and just as there had to be profound changes in how the general population was educated if the country was to retain its position of power, it was clear that a new view of the nation-state was needed if the tensions between the classes were not to spill over into violence. The problem was that the Liberals and the Conservatives were both reluctant to cede too much power to women and the working class, forces that many in their parties viewed as dangerously subversive.

These (and other) forces for change were mobilising outside the Houses of Parliament, and writers such as George Bernard Shaw and H. G. Wells (those mentioned by Birling in J. B. Priestley's *An Inspector Calls*) were articulating for many the need for reform. Ramsey MacDonald became secretary to the Labour Representation Committee (the LRC) at the end of the nineteenth century; the LRC changed its name to the Labour Party in 1906, and in the same year MacDonald, along with 28 other MPs, was elected to the House of Commons to form the Parliamentary Labour Party. The Liberal Party had agreed a 'Progressive Alliance' with the Labour Party, which allowed the new party to put up candidates in seats without standing against Liberals. It was to prove a costly concession by the Liberals.

The rise of the unions

Organised labour — in union or party political forms — was gaining ground. Between 1910 and 1914 serious strikes broke out (among them strikes by miners and dockers), threatening to cripple the country's economy. The strikers demanded better pay and working conditions. Between 1910 and 1911 the country was almost brought to a standstill by the unions, and there was a growing realisation that the more the ruling class depended upon the working man for his wealth, the more powerful the working man became: what he needed was organisation, and that came through the formation of the National Transport Workers' Federation. This laid the foundations for the Transport and General Workers' Union, founded in 1922.

The labour unrest that threatened to destabilise Britain was not restricted to these shores alone. Faulks begins *Birdsong* at a time when France was undergoing similar moments of confrontation; Meyraux, the foreman and head of the 'syndicate', is the embodiment of this new, self-confident working man. The ruling classes of the developed nations of Europe were terrified that the 'spectre' of communism would rock them to their foundations, and although the war stalled that (except in Russia), the high point of unquestioned, class-defined *noblesse oblige* was drawing to a close.

Education

It was not uncommon for the middle and upper classes to employ governesses or nurses to look after their children. Edwardian families were rigidly hierarchical, with

the father being the head of the family, the mother second, and the children very much their inferiors. The distance between adults and children is portrayed in *Birdsong*: Stephen never meets his father and his mother abandons him to his grandfather, who sends him to an orphanage. His guardian, Vaughan, brings Stephen up in a highly utilitarian manner. This generational distance is repeated in Weir's relationship with his father, as well as Azaire's with his children. To some extent the 'healthiest' relationship between father and son is that between Jack and John. The tragedy, of course, is that the war kills this also: when John dies in England his father's life effectively ends.

Some might say that to *not* have a conventionally happy family unit in this novel (Elizabeth is a single parent who gives birth to her married lover's son) is self-serving and tendentious, but Faulks is making a legitimate point: namely that for many the social conventions of the day trapped ordinary, healthy people in impossible situations and forced them to behave in a damaging way, both to themselves and to others. The Edwardians were by no means model parents, but, it could be argued, they were more forward-looking than their forefathers: it was they who passed laws to register all midwives; the first nursery school opened in 1900; school meals were introduced in 1906; special schools for difficult and impoverished children opened in 1908; juvenile courts were introduced, as were borstals, and although these places were grim by modern standards they at least removed children from the danger of having to spend time in adult prisons. In addition, Baden-Powell founded the first Scout camp in 1907.

In 1902 Balfour's Education Act was passed. It was a revolution in the educational system, recognising as it did that if Britain was to remain a world power it could not expect to do so with an uneducated, illiterate workforce. The government created the model for the primary and secondary school system of education, which, like many other Edwardian inventions, was spread around the world through empire. However, most schools, whether grammar or private, remained brutal places, and the teachers employed in them were often uneducated and underpaid. Corporal punishment was routine, and it was a strongly held belief, certainly in the relatively privileged quads of the great public schools, that the duty of any school was to bend and shape the individual into an adult who was prepared to serve, whatever the service demanded. It was an attitude that would serve the country — if not the soldiers — well in the First World War, and it was neatly summed up in Sir Henry Newbolt's famous poem, 'Vitaï Lampada' (the lamp of life), a late Victorian poem that became hugely popular when war broke out.

To be young in Edwardian Britain afforded you with perhaps more opportunities than had ever existed before, but much was dependent on the class you were born into. There were opportunities to improve one's lot (literacy rose year on year at this time, thanks to compulsory education and public libraries), but if you were working class it was almost inevitable that you would end up working in a physically demanding, low-paid job. If you were middle class (and male), however, the world was a different place: a good school, a place at university, a well-paid job: all these were possible, indeed, they were expected. But the war changed all that: the new world order, carefully engineered by men in hats, with thick moustaches and serious faces, was about to be violently shaken, never to return to what it once was.

Women

At the start of the twentieth century Britain was a patriarchal society. When one contemplates sepia-tinted photographs from this era, filled as it is with Larkin's 'fools in old-style hats and coats', what one sees are men dressed almost uniformly in black, and women dressed so that almost every part of their bodies is concealed. Each picture, to our modern eyes, seems to deepen our impression of an age characterised by sombreness and repression. However, sexual expression finds its outlets regardless of the extent of the restrictions, and it was no different in the Edwardian period.

Before the First World War, 'women's work' was routinely domestic. Out of 24 million women, it is estimated that 1.7 million worked in domestic service, 800,000 in textiles and 600,000 in various clothing trades, although the vast majority were expected to stay at home and look after the children and the house.

The British view of women was, at the outbreak of the war, recognisably Victorian: they were idealised, and seen as intrinsically good, incapable of violence, naturally supportive of men, protective, nurturing. A woman, according to *A Little Mother*, a popular pamphlet published in 1916, was 'created for giving life, and men to take it'. For the novelist Virginia Woolf, women had to act as magnifying mirrors 'reflecting the figure of man at twice its natural size. Without that power...the glories of all our wars would be unknown'. We see, in countless visual and literary representations of women, creatures who were passive: they were urged to 'lie back and think of England' when having intercourse with their husbands, a phrase that neatly sums up the relationship a woman was expected to have with both the man and her country. They were, when war broke out, and as countless propaganda posters show, used to blackmail their husbands and sons into behaving 'like men': to go and fight, to not shame them by refusing to fight, to go and 'beat the enemy' in order to protect their wives, mothers and daughters.

However, much of this was to change when, because of the growing shortage of young men, women were called upon to do their work. Society seemed to accept these changes grudgingly, with some trade unions (organisations set up to protect workers' rights) suspicious of this new workforce 'diluting' the trades they sought to protect. Nevertheless, women began to work, for the first time in Britain, alongside men in environments that were often aggressively masculine: they worked in munitions factories, steelworks, mines, they worked on the land harvesting crops, and they cared for the troops when they were sent home injured. Women were not

granted the vote until 1918 — and even then it was for those aged 30 and above — and suffrage was awarded as a way of thanking women for the contribution they made to the Allied victory. Even so, huge progress was made by women over the course of the war towards obtaining true equality in the eyes of the law.

The immense loss that women experienced in these years — seeing their beloved sons, brothers, husbands and fathers killed in conflict — is beyond our imagination. Visit a war memorial in any British town or village and you will see the names of men from the same families killed, often within days of each other. Added to this was the trauma of adapting to the return of loved ones who had been injured, both psychologically and physically, by the war: it was often women who had to look after these men, many of whom had been altered beyond recognition by the battles they had fought.

The First World War

The First World War profoundly altered the world's political landscape and yet it is probably true that most people know surprisingly little about its causes. Sebastian Faulks summed up this opinion when he said in an interview with Margaret Reynolds and Jonathan Noakes (Vintage Living Texts) that 'people of my generation had rather my view: "terrible thing, appalling thing, massive slaughters…whew… you know…" but didn't really know much more than that'. Such sentiments can be found in the modern sections of *Birdsong*, where ignorance of the war is shown in stark contrast with the graphic descriptions of the action (e.g. on p. 256). It is probably also true that to some extent the First World War suffers in comparison with the Second World War. The later conflict is seen as a clear, black-and-white battle of ideologies: democracy versus dictatorship. Taking sides was, morally speaking, straightforward when one was facing the aggressive expansionism of Nazi Germany and Fascist Italy.

Our view of the conflict of 1914 to 1918 is very different: to some extent we see it as a terrible mistake, an avoidable tragedy brought about by a series of ill-advised alliances and prolonged by outdated, entrenched tactics drawn up by arrogant and distant leaders — the donkeys who led the lions. The slaughter in the fields of France and Belgium was so great that it is almost beyond comprehension. The statistics alone tell the story: the Allied forces (the Russian empire, France, the British empire, Italy and, eventually, the United States) lost an estimated 5.1 million men, and the Central Powers (Austria-Hungary, the German empire, the Ottoman empire and Bulgaria) lost some 3.5 million; taken together this works out at nearly 5,500 deaths every day. The Allied powers also had nearly 13 million wounded military personnel, the Central Powers 8.5 million; nearly 8 million were recorded as missing combatants. Many towns and cities were ruined as the fighting swept across borders.

The origins of the war

How could this happen? What most people do know is that the assassination of Archduke Franz Ferdinand, heir to the Austro-Hungarian throne, by Gavrilo Princip, a Bosnian-Serb nationalist, on 28 June 1914, set in motion a series of events that would result, a few weeks later, in the outbreak of the world's first global conflict. The assassination resulted in Austria-Hungary declaring war on Serbia, which in turn dragged in the other powers who had signed alliances to protect each other's interests. There were other reasons for the war: the rise of nationalism in Europe made Princip's action more likely; the alliance system was inherently territorial and confrontational; and it could be argued that if Franz Ferdinand had not been murdered then another incident would have resulted in conflict sooner rather than later.

The major powers, especially Germany and Great Britain, had embarked on a rapid (and financially damaging) arms race that further heightened the tension in Europe. Added to these factors was a scramble for overseas markets — in particular the Far East — which meant that economic growth had to be aggressively pursued, often with military 'protection'. Many — including Vladimir Lenin (who eventually led Russia out of the war) — believed that the economic system of the time was the principal reason for war: markets had to be protected at all costs. Consequently, the main European powers engaged not only in a battle for the domination of Europe but, as they were imperial powers, to extend their empires as well. There was also a large degree of pride involved in heightening this conflict: nobody was prepared to back down because to do so would be to risk national humiliation and economic hardship. There were old scores to settle as well: France wanted revenge on Germany for its annexing of the provinces of Alsace and Lorraine in the Franco-Prussian war of 1870; Germany wanted revenge on France for taking Morocco at the beginning of the twentieth century.

Germany's Schlieffen Plan made its expansionist aims clear to everybody — it was preparing to fight on both its western and eastern flanks. Integral to this plan was the quick defeat of France and Belgium (on its Western Front). Germany's decision to build a navy, which it hoped would threaten Great Britain's, was blatantly confrontational. France and Russia had similarly aggressive military plans in place, both of which included seizing German land.

Such a climate goes some way to explaining why the Austro-Hungarian government used the assassination for its own ends: it knew that the ultimatum given to Serbia, containing impossible demands, could not be met, and that the only possible outcome would be war. Serbia had an alliance with Russia; for the Schlieffen Plan to work Germany had to attack France and Belgium before Russia. It declared war on Russia on 1 August and, two days later, on France. Germany's leader, Kaiser Wilhelm II, ordered German troops to attack Belgium and then France; this in turn brought Great Britain into the war as a consequence of its treaty commitment to defend the independence of Belgium.

Thousands of books have been written about the war. However, a brief overview is necessary to place *Birdsong* into some sort of context. *Birdsong* is very concerned with trench warfare: the descriptions of the living (and dying) conditions that the soldiers had to endure are graphic and unflinching, and many consider Faulks's intensely powerful depiction of the Battle of the Somme as the artistic highpoint of the novel.

The first modern war

The First World War saw the introduction of new, lethal military devices: barbed wire, machine guns, poison gas and the tank were all employed with devastating effect by both sides. The war transformed the world. Oliver Stone wrote:

> In four years, the world went from 1870 to 1940. In 1914, cavalry cantered off to stirring music…Fortresses were readied for prolonged sieges, medical services were still quite primitive, and severely wounded men were likely to die. By 1918, matters had become very different, and French generals had already devised a new method of warfare, in which tanks, infantry, and aircraft collaborated, in the manner of the German *Blitzkrieg* ('lightning war' of 1940).
>
> *World War One: A Short History,* Allen Lane, 2007, p. 29.

As the numbers of casualties increased, both sides began to literally dig themselves into fixed positions: moving was too dangerous, and so a war of attrition became established. The more entrenched they became, the more static the fighting; any progress on either side came at a heavy price. The names of the battles have passed into a collective memory, acting as shorthand for mass slaughter: Passchendaele, Verdun, Albert, Vimy Ridge, Arras, Ypres and, most infamously, the Battle of the Somme. In this battle, which started on 1 July 1916, 1,508,652 shells were fired in the week before the assault began; the British army suffered over 57,000 casualties in one day, of which nearly 20,000 died. The maximum distance taken on the first day of fighting, at the village of Montauban, was 1,200 yards.

The war dragged on without any decisive breakthrough. But in 1917 two events changed its course. First, the new Bolshevik government in Russia, led by Lenin, withdrew from the war. The treaty they signed continues to be controversial because it ceded Germany so much land: Germany gained massive areas of eastern Europe and was able to redeploy many of its troops to the Western Front. Second, pressure on the president of the United States, Woodrow Wilson, to enter the war came to a head when German U-boats sank seven US merchant ships over a short period of time. The Americans were finding it increasingly difficult to remain neutral. The USA was not the superpower it would later become but even so its declaration of war on the Central Powers, on 6 April 1917, had huge consequences: it was able to send millions of men to the Western Front, thus neutralising the benefits of German disengagement from the Eastern Front.

A turning point

The battle at Amiens drastically changed the direction of the war. Allied troops employed hundreds of new tanks to cut through the barbed wire set by the Germans. In one offensive they advanced seven miles in seven hours. Further south, several days later, at Albert, the German army was pushed back 34 miles in a matter of days; psychologically it was extremely damaging because they were back to their starting point of 1914 — the Hindenburg Line. In territorial terms they had achieved nothing.

American and Commonwealth forces were, by 1917, overwhelming German resistance (the USA alone was sending 10,000 men a day to Europe). Coupled with falling industrial output at home, the German forces' morale was very low, and the Allied forces capitalised on this with relentless assaults. Germany had no choice but to seek an end to the war: Wilson demanded the abdication of the Kaiser, and with it came the end of imperial Germany. With the defeat of Germany the Central Powers collapsed almost immediately: first Bulgaria, then the Ottoman empire, and finally the Austro-Hungarian empire surrendered to the Allied forces. On the eleventh hour of the eleventh day of the eleventh month a ceasefire came into effect.

Peace — but not a lasting one

The Treaty of Versailles marked both the formal cessation of conflict, as well as the end of four empires: the German, the Austro-Hungarian, the Ottoman and the Russian. In purely political terms the most lasting consequences of the war were the enormous war reparations that Germany was forced to pay to the victorious powers; the nationalist movement led by the Nazi party exploited the overwhelming sense of grievance felt by ordinary Germans who saw that the ongoing, crippling financial burden would continue to hamper any hope of their country recovering from the terrible conflict. To add insult to injury, Germany was forced to accept responsibility for the war.

The full consequences of the First World War can only be guessed at: we can look to the history books and see how countries emerged or died in this terrible theatre of conflict, and we can read about the effects the war had on those who took part in it through the many letters and poems written at the time. Ninety years on, it is still impossible to comprehend the impact of this first global war. Nothing can tell us of what we lost: the poets, musicians, artists, scientists and politicians, most unknown, who died before they had realised their full potential; or just the ordinary men who would, if they had lived, have gone on to be, like Jack Firebrace, good and caring fathers to children who would remain forever unborn. Faulks describes this sense of the unfulfilled potential at the end of the Battle of the Somme (p. 236):

> Price was reading the roll call. Before him were standing the men from his company who had managed to return. Their faces were shifty and grey in the dark.

To begin with he asked after the whereabouts of each missing man. After a time he saw that it would take too long. Those who had survived were not always sure whom they had seen dead...

Price began to speed the process. He hurried from one unanswered name to the next. Byrne, Hunt, Jones, Tipper, Wood, Leslie, Barnes, Studd, Richardson, Savile, Thompson, Hodgson, Birkenshaw, Llewellyn, Francis, Arkwright, Duncan, Shea, Simons, Anderson, Blum, Fairbrother. Names came pattering into the dusk, bodying out the places of their forebears, the villages and towns where the telegrams would be delivered, the houses where the blinds would be drawn, where low moans would come in the afternoon behind closed doors; and the places that had borne them, which would be like nunneries, like dead towns without their life or purpose, without the sound of fathers and their children, without young men at the factories or in the fields, with no husbands for the women, no deep sound of voices in the inns, with the children who would have been born, who would have grown and worked or painted, or even governed, left ungenerated in their fathers' shattered flesh that lay in stinking shellholes in the beet-crop soil, leaving their homes to put up only granite slabs in place of living flesh, on whose inhuman surface the moss and lichen would cast their crawling green indifference.

Many have argued that the causes of the Second World War can be found in the First World War: certainly it fostered in Germany a sense of resentment that made the rise of Hitler and Nazism inevitable: he promised the German people a renewed sense of self-belief, and the desire to right the wrongs of Versailles meant that within the space of a generation the world was drawn, once again, into a devastating conflict.

Trench warfare

> To-night, this frost will fasten on this mud and us,
> Shrivelling many hands, puckering foreheads crisp.
> The burying-party, picks and shovels in shaking grasp,
> Pause over half-known faces. All their eyes are ice,
>   But nothing happens.

The last verse of 'Exposure' by Wilfred Owen

Many men joined up at the start of the war because they were promised that it 'would all be over by Christmas'; they also perhaps visualised a war of derring-do, dashing about on horseback, or shooting the Germans from a safe distance. It was impressed upon them that to fight was their duty, but the dangers involved were both concealed and, to a great extent, unknown. There were added attractions and incentives: many joined the army because they were promised that they would serve alongside their friends and work colleagues (these became known as the 'Pals Battalions'); many also joined because it provided some regular pay and an escape from the drudgery of their work. General Sir Henry Rawlinson, who was in charge of the British IV Corps at the outbreak of war, rightly argued that more men would volunteer if they knew the people they were going to fight alongside. Large groups of men from places as diverse as dockyards and public schools formed distinct battalions. The tactic was, in many ways, a resounding success: by the end of September 1914 over 750,000 men had enlisted; by January 1915 it had risen to 1 million. Out of nearly 1,000 battalions formed between 1914 and 1916, two-thirds were Pals Battalions. But the cost to local communities when these men were killed was huge.

When we think of the war we tend to think of the trenches. Trench warfare began in September 1914 and ended in 1918. This partly explains why the war dragged on for so long: there was little movement from either side, and what movement there was came at great cost, as battles like the Somme and Ypres show. Men had to survive not only the bombs, bullets and gas attacks of the enemy but, as their diaries and letters home testify, they also had to withstand appalling weather conditions and infestations of rats and other parasites.

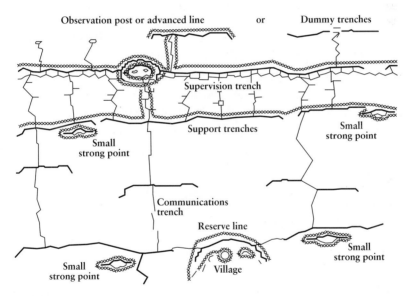

A typical trench system from 1916

Disease, especially trench fever, which was similar to influenza, was spread by lice. They bred in the seams of uniforms and the soldiers complained of constant itching. Worse, though, were the rats. These flourished in the mud, water and waste: they fed on the corpses, in turn spreading disease; they ate through vital rations; they even nibbled through communication wires, putting the men at the Front at even greater risk because they were cut off from their headquarters unless they repaired the damage. Diseases such as dysentery spread because of poor hygiene: toilet facilities were basic and the buckets used often spilled into the trenches. Men often simply relieved themselves in shell holes, consequently infecting the water supply.

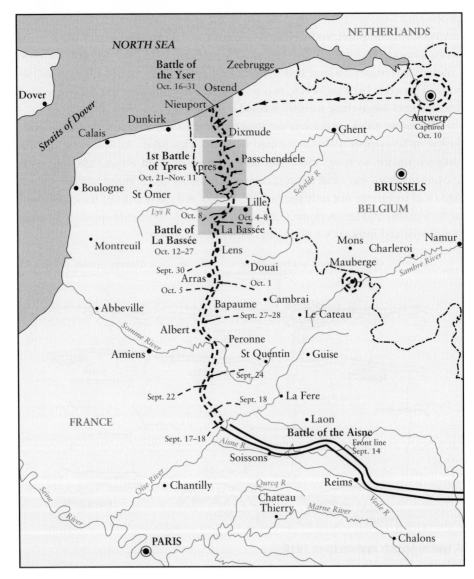

The Western Front, 1914

The rations that the field kitchens provided were, as the war dragged on, often barely enough to keep a man alive: biscuits, corned beef, tea, some bread and jam. This was the staple diet of the British Army and almost none of it was fresh.

The trenches, particularly the British ones, which were not as well built as the German trenches, frequently flooded. The men often had to stand for hours waist deep in freezing water, which could result in the dreaded trench foot and in some cases amputation. The winter of 1916–17 in France and Flanders was the coldest in living memory, and many died of exposure.

Duty and discipline

A typical 'Tommy' (the **colloquial** term for a private in the army) would be expected to serve for four days at the front line, followed by four days in 'close reserve' (behind the front line but ready to reinforce the line when needed), followed by four days at rest. Such a rotation could not be guaranteed and many men stayed at the Front for much longer periods. One unit would replace another, rather than individuals being replaced one by one (although this did happen for numerous reasons). Soldiers had various duties to perform once at the front line, including keeping watch: they would listen and look for any activity across No Man's Land, a job that could be both extremely dangerous and very tedious. If they fell asleep on duty they could be tried, and for such an offence the soldier in question could be shot. Under cover of darkness small groups of men were sent out to repair barbed wire (a recent and despised invention), or to recover the dead. They also had to repair the crumbling trenches. Each company of men had a commanding officer to whom they would report every hour, and it was his job to ensure that the rota of work was being enforced and that his men were prepared to attack or respond at short notice. All those at the front line had to wear their equipment at all times, with bayonets fixed. No man could leave his post without permission from his commanding officer.

The British Army was ruthless in maintaining discipline, and numerous charges brought against a soldier could result in the death penalty. The table below gives some examples of charges and penalties that a soldier could expect.

Charge	Penalty
Doing violence to a person bringing provisions to the forces	Death
When acting as a sentinel on active service, sleeping at his post	Death
Striking a superior officer	Death
Committing an offence against a resident in the country in which the soldier was serving	Death
Leaving the ranks on pretence of taking wounded men to the rear	Penal servitude
Leaving his CO to go in search of plunder	Death
Misbehaving before the enemy in such a manner as to show cowardice	Death

Those who survived the war did so by adapting to these harsh conditions: they established routines, made friends, sang songs, played football, wrote letters home, read books and newspapers (which could be delivered by special request), kept pets (including rats), embroidered, smoked cigarettes, told jokes, went on leave back to 'blighty' (England) and got drunk; they even tried to make their trenches homely, giving them place names such as Lovers Lane, Lavender Walk, Idiots Corner, Chaos Trench, Gangrene Alley — each showing a bleak but necessary sense of humour. They did everything they could to remain human, and it is often surprising to see how

'normal' life was for many of them. Perhaps the most famous episode of mankind's willingness to resort to a familiar routine — despite the circumstances — came on Christmas Day 1915 on the Western Front. In some of the trenches there was a spontaneous outbreak of peace, with soldiers from both sides ceasing hostilities: they clambered out of their trenches, exchanged cigarettes, drank cognac, ate, joked, and even played football together. The commanding officers were worried, however, that such informal truces would lower morale and soon ended such activities: they argued that it is harder to kill somebody you know than it is to kill a stranger.

The British Army

Although Great Britain was a global power at the end of the nineteenth century its army was surprisingly small. Successive British governments had poured money into the Royal Navy rather than its land forces, believing that the empire could only be protected through naval power. Until the Germans began their programme of military expansion, the British had remained detached from Europe, maintaining that the empire was the first priority. As the clouds of conflict began to darken the European skies it became increasingly clear that the old dependency on sea power, important though it was, would have to change, and that resources would have to be directed into the army. The unexpectedly difficult and prolonged Boer War, which the British had won but at tremendous cost, both in human and financial terms, exposed a land force that could be beaten by a relatively unsophisticated (but highly motivated) enemy.

The British Army, which numbered about a quarter of a million troops, was a professional force, and it was supported by several hundred thousand reservists and members of the territorial forces. Even so, it was no match for German land forces. With the outbreak of war numbers had to rapidly expand if the British were going to help the French stop Germany. By 1915, 29 new divisions had been added to the existing army's forces, bringing in over 2 million more soldiers; in 1916 conscription was introduced, which added an additional 2 million men. However, the British, like their European counterparts, had to adjust to the new tactics being employed on the battlefields of Belgium and northern France: the horses that had served in the Boer and Crimea conflicts would be either shot down by the new machine guns or snarled up in barbed wire. The First World War, more than anything else, forced the British Army to become a modern fighting machine.

The structure of the army

The British Army was (and is) made up of divisions and brigades — a tactical unit that can change depending on circumstances. Each brigade consists of battalions from different regiments, and these are far more permanent in nature. The regiment is the single most important unit in a soldier's life: each is responsible for recruitment and training, and many of the regiments have their own traditions dating back, in some cases, centuries. In the First World War whole battalions were recruited from the same geographical area, which meant that there was a recognisable regional identity to each regiment, and this in turn contributed to the *esprit de corps*, so important in difficult circumstances. The main drawback to this is that if a regiment loses a lot of men — as happened in both world wars — local communities are devastated by the losses as they are concentrated in one area.

The British Army was engaged in active service for the whole of the First World War, and for much of that time it was entrenched in the Western Front. However, British soldiers fought in every area of the conflict, suffering heavy casualties. Few doubt the bravery of the 'Tommy' (as the British soldiers were called) in this conflict, but had it not been for the support of forces from Commonwealth and empire countries, not to mention the USA, the British would not have been able to stop the march of the highly trained German forces. At the outset of the war Kaiser Wilhelm had dismissed the British Army as 'contemptible'; at the end of the war its reputation had been transformed and it was viewed as a formidable opponent, but this had been achieved at great cost. Germany would not underestimate Britain again.

The war in brief

1914

- 28 June — assassination of Archduke Franz Ferdinand in Sarajevo
- 23 July — Austro-Hungarian ultimatum to Serbia
- 28 July — Austria-Hungary declares war on Serbia
- 1 August — Germany declares war on Russia
- 2 August — German ultimatum to Belgium
- 3 August — Germany declares war on France
- 4 August — Germany invades Belgium. Britain declares war on Germany
- 10 August — Britain declares war on Austria-Hungary
- 23 August — Japan declares war on Germany
- 7 November — British forces land in Mesopotamia
- 25 December — unofficial truce between British and German soldiers on the Western Front

1915

- 7 May — the passenger liner *Lusitania* is sunk off Ireland, with 1,200 lives lost
- 23 May — Italy declares war on Austria-Hungary
- 31 May — London attacked from the air by German Zeppelins
- 1 June — women employed by British munitions factories for the first time
- 6–9 August — Anzac offensive at Gallipoli
- 25 August — Austro-German forces capture Brest-Litovsk

- 23 September   Bulgaria joins the war in support of the Central Powers
- 25 September   Battle of Loos, a Franco–British offensive against the Germans, begins
- 6 October   Austro-German forces invade Serbia
- 8 October   Austrian forces capture Belgrade
- 11 October   Bulgarian forces invade Serbia
- 19 December   evacuation of Allied forces from Gallipoli

1916
- 25 January   introduction of conscription in Britain for single men (extended to married men on 16 May)
- 21 February   Battle of Verdun — a key German offensive — starts (and ends on 18 December)
- 31 May   Battle of Jutland — the major naval battle of the war — begins
- 1 July   Battle of the Somme begins (and ends on 18 November)
- 27 August   Romania joins the war in support of the Allies
- 7 December   David Lloyd George replaces Asquith as British Prime Minister

1917
- 11 March   British forces capture Baghdad
- 12 March   The Russian Revolution begins
- 15 March   Tsar Nicholas II abdicates
- 3 April   Lenin returns to Russia with help from German forces
- 6 April   USA declares war on Germany
- 31 July   Battle of Passchendaele begins (and ends on 10 November)
- 6 November   Clemenceau becomes French Prime Minister
- 15 December   Russia signs armistice with Germany

1918
- 1 April   Creation of the RAF
- 7 April   Meat rationing introduced across Britain
- 8 August   Battle of Amiens begins
- 21 August   Battle of Albert begins
- 3 November   Austria-Hungary signs armistice with the Allies
- 9 November   Kaiser Wilhelm II abdicates
- 11 November   Germany signs armistice with the Allies

The literature of the First World War

In political terms Europe was relatively stable between the end of the Franco-Prussian War (1871) and the outbreak of the First World War. In many ways, the majority of the growing middle class enjoyed a period of unparalleled prosperity at this time. Although the working classes of every industrialised nation probably did not view it the same way, the hardships experienced in the rapid process of industrialisation were, for many at the beginning of the twentieth century, starting to bring rewards. Businessmen travelled across Europe by train, and there was very little bureaucracy to worry about. This new internationalism — so often seen as the preserve of the late twentieth century — can be seen in *Birdsong* through the character of Stephen Wraysford: he travels from England to observe the working practices of the French industrialised classes. Behind this new openness, however, lay the organised unrest promoted by the European trade union movement (and personified in Meyraux, the foreman and head of the union), which was campaigning for better pay and conditions for the working class. Although the war interrupted such agitation in many countries, it erupted into revolution in Russia in 1917 and threatened to spread elsewhere.

It was in the arts that the *belle époque* found its lasting legacy. In art this period saw the growing acceptance of Impressionism and later Expressionism, both of which were partial rejections of romantic and conservative artistic schools of the nineteenth century. Painters such as Monet and Degas experimented with materials as well as methods, and this desire to reinvent and re-present the physical world so that it was seen to be to a great extent a projection of individual perceptual experience would reach its apogee in the Modernist movement of postwar Europe. In literature, writers such as Maupassant and Zola in France, and H. G. Wells, Henry James, Kipling, Conrad and Shaw in Great Britain, described the age in new and challenging ways.

War poetry and Owen

It is the poetry of the First World War that remains its most enduring literary legacy. The works of Sassoon, Rosenberg, Edward Thomas, Rupert Brook and, perhaps most famously of all, Wilfred Owen, define a generation's experience of this conflict. Owen's poetry is visceral in its power: seething with controlled rage, graphic in its descriptions of the scenes he saw at the Front — but always instilled with an acute intelligence that avoided simplistic and reductive negative propaganda — Owen's poetry is great literature in its own right.

He wrote many memorable poems — 'Anthem for Doomed Youth', 'Exposure', 'Futility' and 'Disabled' among them, but perhaps his most famous poem is 'Dulce Et Decorum Est'. The poem consists of 28 lines, written in a rather loose iambic pentameter. It describes a gas attack on a group of soldiers and the rush of the men to protect themselves from this new form of warfare. One in their number drops his mask, and the image of him 'guttering, choking, drowning' powerfully describes his painful death. The final lines of the poem, 'Dulce et decorum est/Pro patria mori', addressed to the propagandist Jessie Pope, confront 'the old lie' used to persuade young men to risk their lives: namely, 'it is sweet and fitting to die for one's country'.

Owen's poem was published posthumously in 1920. He was killed on 4 November 1918 — exactly one week before the signing of the Armistice — attempting, with the rest of his 'D' company, a crossing of the Sambre-Oise Canal at Ors. He was 25. He was promoted to the rank of lieutenant the day after his death; to add even greater sadness to this terrible episode Owen's mother received notification of his death as the church bells were ringing out to mark the end of the war. His poetry continues to be studied because it has real literary merit, but also because it articulates an authentic voice from the trenches: Owen — like Sassoon — knew what the war meant, and as such it carries greater resonance, in many ways, than the work of those who wrote about it from a distance.

The First World War novel

For any writer — novelist, poet, historian or critic — who wishes to write about the First World War (or the Great War as it was referred to at the time) there is one obvious problem: how do you make your work original and distinctive? The conflict of 1914–18 was unusual for many reasons. First, the casualties were unprecedented and remain almost impossible to comprehend (over 15 million are estimated to have died). Second, it was the first truly modern war: tanks, aeroplanes, machine guns, barbed wire, gas, landmines — the ghastly litany of familiar methods of destruction were tested in the fields of northern Europe in this conflict (hence the appalling loss of life) and they have stayed with us ever since. The First World War was also the first war covered by what we now know as 'the media'. It was the first conflict to be filmed (for reasons of propaganda as much as reportage). War correspondents sent reports back to their papers via telegram and war photographers captured action on the Front. It also inspired literature of unprecedented intensity and quality. In the age of satellite television, the internet and mobile phones we are used to watching conflicts as they unfold, but the First World War saw the beginnings of this process: we are familiar with the poetry of writers such as Sassoon, Owen, Brooke and Rosenberg (among many others), but behind them there is a wealth of photographic, aural, oral and written records that threaten to overwhelm — and to some extent invalidate — all subsequent voices.

First-hand accounts

Although the war is most closely associated with poetry, it did produce much else that is worth reading. Henri Barbusse's novel *Under Fire* was published in 1917 (and translated into English in 1918). It is one of the first novels of the conflict and was based on Barbusse's own experiences. It is set entirely in France and is unflinching in its description of life in the trenches. It influenced Owen and Sassoon, and is regarded by many as a classic of the **genre**. Geoff Dyer, in *The Missing of the Somme*, quotes the following passage as particularly important because it looks ahead to how the war will be remembered — as well as forgotten and changed — by subsequent generations:

> We shall forget!…Not only the length of the big misery, which can't be reckoned, as you say, ever since the beginning, but the marches that turn up the ground and turn it up again…we shall forget not only those, but even the foul wounds of the shells and machine-guns, the mines, the gas, and the counter-attacks. At those moments you're full of excitement of reality, and you've some satisfaction. But all that wears off and goes away, you don't know how and you don't know where, but there's only the names left…

Remembering those names, if not the lives and experiences behind them, becomes a duty for a nation which promises, every November, that we 'shall never forget'. Novels are part of that attempted, ongoing remembrance, and the writer can do much to fill in the blanks. Rebecca West's short novel *The Return of the Soldier* was published in 1918 (and set in 1916) and raises the difficult subject of shell shock: Chris Baldry returns to England suffering from amnesia and is looked after by three women he once loved. Jenny, his cousin and narrator, articulates a deeply held lament for a lost innocence and, indeed, a lost England.

Perhaps the most famous novel of the period is Erich Maria Remarque's *Im Westen nichts Neues* (*All Quiet on the Western Front*), published in 1929 (translated into English in 1930). It described the war (from a German perspective) in unflinching detail, and it became an international bestseller and an acclaimed film. It is narrated by Paul Bäumer, a 19-year-old writer, and is critical of the campaign and the damage it did to both individuals and society: at its heart is an exploration of the growing sense of dehumanisation the soldiers feel as they are caught up in a process they are unable to influence.

Remarque's novel is unusual because, unlike many of those written at the same time, it continues to be read and studied today. Another such novel is *A Farewell to Arms* (1929) by the American novelist, Ernest Hemingway. Again, like so many novels written about this period, it is semi-autobiographical. The story is narrated by Lieutenant Frederic Henry, an American ambulance driver serving in the Italian Army in the First World War, who falls in love with Catherine. At its heart the novel is a love story, set against the backdrop of the war.

Second-hand accounts

So graphic and lastingly moving are many of these first-hand accounts of the trenches that one has to ask what can possibly be added to our understanding of this conflict by writers who did not experience it first hand? To put it simply: why read Sebastian Faulks when one can read Wilfred Owen and Edward Thomas? It is not an easy question to answer, but it is worth considering, since what art form other than literature can unify so many experiences into one **narrative**? The many voices of the First World War are individual perspectives and, as such, are fragments of an impossibly complex picture. A writer can attempt to bring many of these together and seek to present the personal and the political. Faulks himself is aware of these

problems and is honest, both about how the writer can prepare for the task as well as the liberating effect that not being personally involved in the conflict can have:

> I think that many novels were written by officers about ten years later and are really memoirs offered with a degree of self-protective irony. *Birdsong* is a very head-on, unironic book. It holds nothing back. Also it tells it from the ordinary man's point of view. It is more of a novel, with the full novelistic palette, than those elegant, restrained memoirs. It has women and children and families, themes, sub-plots etc. Most first war novels are not really novels at all but memoirs and I think that is perhaps where *Birdsong* fits in.

> My paternal grandfather was too old to fight, my maternal grandfather did fight but was killed in WWII so I never met him. I did talk to various veterans and got some feeling from them. It was good to stand in the mud with men who had been there. One of them held my hand as he described what had happened and through him I felt connected, physically, to the experience. But most of my research was from contemporary documents in the Imperial War Museum. I prefer to work from documents. Documents don't lie. They always remember. They don't get drunk at lunch time and fall asleep. Mostly, however — and I cannot over-emphasise the importance of this function to the novelist — I made it up.

> Source: www.randomhouse.co.uk/readersgroup/qanda0401.htm

A writer can only hope to deepen our understanding of this thoroughly documented war if he or she is able to bring something new to the subject. Faulks does this by adding a distinctly modern emotional and psychological force to existing narratives. His text is informed with the lessons of history, and it presents the subject matter with the seriousness it deserves without avoiding asking difficult questions about the nature of war and the effects it has on society and the individuals that comprise it. It could be argued that those who are outside the tumult, but living with the consequences of the war, are as entitled to explore and interpret it as those who took part.

The resurgence of interest in the First World War novel in this country can be attributed to Pat Barker and Sebastian Faulks. Barker's trilogy (*Regeneration*, 1990, *The Eye in the Door*, 1993, and *The Ghost Road*, 1995) coincided with Faulks's *Birdsong* (1993).

Freud and the beginning of Modernism

Modernism

Modernism has no clear definition or period. One reason for this is that it was not a movement restricted to one genre: it ranged across literature, music, art and architecture and was, in many ways, a response to a variety of political and economic events in many different countries. Added to this, Modernism reached different peaks at different times within these countries: indeed, it could be argued that it was the dominant cultural tendency in France between the 1890s and 1940s, and the same could be said about Modernism in England from the beginning of the twentieth century and Germany from the 1890s to the 1920s. Different periods could be applied to Modernism in the USA and Russia. Roughly speaking though, it could be said that Modernism lasted in Europe between 1890 and the outbreak of the Second World War in 1939. **Postmodernism** is a term more often encountered after this date, but it would be a mistake to assume that the 'rise' of Postmodernism saw Modernism superseded: they both coexist (if they can be comfortably distinguished at all, which many critics question).

The First World War complicates the picture still further: some believe that the fragmentation of society that the war precipitated increased the momentum of Modernism; others believe that the war interrupted and possibly even derailed its development. To add further complications to any one clear definition, one has to accept that within such a loosely termed movement are other movements pertaining to different periods including Surrealism, Formalism, Structuralism, Dadaism, Existentialism, Expressionism, Futurism, Symbolism and Vorticism. What we can say is that Modernism marked a break with the past: each artist who contributed to the movement questioned the established rules and they often did so by using innovative forms of expression. It would have been impossible to imagine the Victorians understanding the literary forms explored by, among others, T. S. Eliot and James Joyce, although the origins of more abstract — and less **figurative** — art forms can be found in the work of artists of the nineteenth century (most notably Turner and Whistler). Modernist artists in art, literature, music and architecture could trace their influences back to the nineteenth century and beyond: it is a domino theory of effect. The difference was that they deliberately subverted many of the rules they had absorbed in order to represent a very changed world in a way that would reflect its new condition. As the *Oxford English Dictionary* states, Modernism can be 'generally characterised by a deliberate break with classical and traditional forms or methods of expression'.

Many factors influenced Modernism, most obviously new research in psychoanalysis and the politics of the left, especially those of Marx and Engels. It would, for example, be impossible to fully appreciate the theatre of Bertolt Brecht (1898–1956) or the art of George Grosz (1893–1959) without an understanding of the political context in which they worked: politics, economics, philosophy and psychoanalysis all contributed to make the period before and after the First World War uniquely combustible.

Sigmund Freud

One figure who had a lasting and radical effect on mankind's view of himself is Sigmund Freud (1856–1939). A distinction must be made here between psychoanalysis (a term coined by Freud) and literary psychoanalysis. In modern novels such

as *Birdsong* by Sebastian Faulks and the *Regeneration* trilogy by Pat Barker, characters are clearly viewed through the lens of modern psychoanalysis, and frequently explicitly so, but this was not necessarily the case at the time the novels were set. Modern writers and readers in the West live, to varying degrees, with a legacy of **Freudian** thought.

Of particular interest when studying the literature of this period are Freud's theories of the ego, the super-ego, and the id. Freud developed the concept of a 'psychic apparatus' in 1923, which was late in his career. He felt that the human psyche could be divided into these three parts: the uncoordinated and impulsive urges can be termed the 'id'; the 'super-ego' represents the ideal and is inherently moralistic; the 'ego' balances these two extremes, and is often manifested in the individual's behaviour: it is realistic and organised. It is relatively easy to apply such concepts to nations as well as individuals, especially when we view something as extreme as the war. The id was described by Freud in the *New Introductory Lectures on Psychoanalysis* (1933) as 'the dark, inaccessible part of our personality'; it is child-like, and a child is dominated by the id. The action of taking a nation to war can be seen as an expression of the id: aggressive and short-termist, an outward expression of the uncivilised. The ego, 'what may be called reason and common sense', attempts to reign in the id. The ego is the conscious self, the part that is aware of the madness of the id and is able to judge it, control it, plan it and synthesise it with the super-ego. It is the super-ego that acts as the conscience; it provides the ideals, the goals, the (often unconscious) inherited models we as individuals and as a society reach for. So the First World War, like all wars, can be seen as a massive externalisation of an inner conflict: the id running rampant before the ego can assert its sense of order.

Applying Freud's concepts to literature can be illuminating, and it is clear that in much of the literature of the First World War the characters described can be seen to be fighting with inner demons that neatly correspond to the id, ego and super-ego. But it is up to the student to decide how far to interpret the writers' aims in a way that can also, if employed too many times, be unnecessarily self-limiting.

Freud's influence on modern Western thought is immense. The poet W. H. Auden wrote, in an obituary poem, that 'to us he is no more a person/now but a whole climate of opinion/under whom we conduct our different lives:/Like weather he can only hinder or help'. Auden's contention is that Freud irrevocably changed our way of looking at ourselves and each other: the language, references, images, interpretations — nothing relating to our emotional lives remained untouched by Freud. Indeed, experience itself, be it in an extreme form (as in neurasthenia or shell shock) or something more prosaic, can be understood through Freudian psychoanalysis. Undoubtedly though, Freud's influence has declined, perhaps more in the field of psychoanalysis than in academic and cultural spheres. However, the work he did exploring the subconscious self continues to be relevant to many today, even those who have not read Freud himself.

Chapter summaries

Part One: France 1910

pp. 3–17

The novel begins with a long passage describing the Azaires' house in Amiens. Stephen Wraysford, a young man from England, has arrived to learn about the manufacturing process at Azaire's factory. The family consist of René, Isabelle, Lisette and Grégoire. The atmosphere in the dining room is tense, with Azaire being condescending towards his wife and Lisette, who is 16, flirting with Stephen. After dinner Monsieur and Madame Bérard join them to play cards. When Stephen retires to bed he hears René beating his wife, Isabelle.

pp. 18–33

In the next section Stephen visits the factory, but is immediately aware that it, like the Azaires' home, is filled with tension. Meyraux, the foreman and head of the union, is suspicious of him and anyone associated with management.

Stephen becomes increasingly interested in Isabelle. He studies her, but cannot understand how she can be the mother of two children. After engaging her in conversation he learns that she is the stepmother of both, and that she is René's second wife. Stephen tells her that he knows how her husband treats her, but her response is not favourable: she is embarrassed and ashamed.

Stephen is not discouraged by this reaction; indeed, he becomes more and more fascinated by her, observing her closely. By chance he sees her walking alone one day and decides to follow her and approaches her just as she is about to enter a nondescript property. Isabelle explains that she is bringing food to the workers who can barely afford to live. There is a hint of attraction between the most charismatic of the workers, Lucien Lebrun, and Isabelle, and it is perhaps for this reason that as she leaves the apartment Stephen impulsively kisses her on the cheek.

pp. 34–47

We then learn more about Isabelle. Her life has not been a happy one: the youngest of five daughters, Isabelle was close to only one of them: Jeanne. Her parents were distant and cold. She had a brief, but doomed, love affair with a soldier named Jean Destournel, but this was ended by her father, and it was also her father who introduced her to Azaire. The courting is described in terms of a business arrangement and it is clear that there is no love between the two.

Stephen seems to be becoming more a part of the Azaire family. He goes on a boat trip with them to the water-gardens on the River Somme. His desire for Isabelle continues to grow: he notices that she does not move her leg away from his in the boat, and it seems to burn into him. Isabelle, however, remains aloof and distant.

pp. 48–62

Tensions begin to rise, both in the factory and at home. Stephen is contacted by his company in London requesting that he return to England; he writes back asking for an extension, claiming that he needs more time to complete his study, but the truth is that he cannot leave Isabelle. The situation in the factory is deteriorating: the workers want to go on strike, and in one meeting a man accuses Lebrun of being too close to Isabelle Azaire. A fight breaks out and Stephen punches the man who makes the accusation.

It is thought advisable that Stephen stay at home for a few days, but in that time he only gets closer to Isabelle. Over lunch one day he kisses her and she runs away, shocked at his boldness, but she returns soon after and invites him to follow her to the red room. Here they make love.

They make love the next day as well, and become more emotionally intimate; Isabelle confesses to Stephen that her husband beats her because he feels inadequate: he cannot father a child with her and his violence acts as a form of arousal for him. She feels sorry for him, and she tells Stephen that his doing this humiliates him rather than her.

pp. 63–117

Their affair is not suspected by René, and the following week the whole family go on a fishing trip. Lisette, who appears to be a sexually precocious 16-year-old, finds Stephen alone and tells him that she knows about the affair. She tries to seduce him, but soon becomes frightened as he, despite himself, begins to get aroused. He scares her into promising that she will not tell anybody about the affair.

The two lovers discuss their plans together and Stephen decides to stay in France. One evening René returns home with the news that the strike has been averted. He also says that he has heard rumours that Isabelle is having an affair with Lebrun. Isabelle tells him that her lover is not Lebrun but Stephen and after a bitter argument Stephen and Isabelle leave the house. They travel to Amiens and then, later, further south.

Several months later Isabelle discovers she is pregnant, but decides not to tell Stephen. Although happy at the prospect of becoming a mother she is uncertain about her relationship with Stephen and she expresses these concerns to her sister, Jeanne, in a letter. She decides that the affair they had was wrong and she leaves Stephen (and stays with Jeanne) in order to think about the future. Her departure devastates Stephen, and although he continues with his menial work he is, inwardly, made cold by her decision to leave. He shuts himself off from others.

Part Two: France 1916

pp. 121–44

We are still in France, but it is a different world. From the peace and quiet of prewar rural France we are transported underground. Jack Firebrace is tunnelling to plant a bomb as close to the German lines as possible. While the men are digging a noise is heard. Jack, famed for his excellent hearing, tells the others that it is shell-fire, but moments later a huge explosion kills three men. Jack returns to his trench, partly blaming himself for what has happened, but he is told by his colleagues that nobody could have done more. He reads a letter from his wife, Margaret, and she tells him that their boy, John, is seriously ill. Jack goes on sentry duty and falls asleep, which is punishable by death by firing squad. He is discovered by two officers: Captain Michael Weir and another man who we later discover is Stephen (now Lieutenant Wraysford). Jack returns to try to sleep and prays to God that he is not court-martialled.

The next day Jack Firebrace reports to Weir. Stephen is there because he commands the infantry platoon that Weir's sappers are working with to destroy German tunnellers. Because Stephen is not Jack's CO he cannot take any action and so Jack avoids charges. Stephen inspects the tunnel that Jack and his men are building.

The miners' routines are described in detail: once relieved of being on duty they bathe, sleep, eat and drink wine at a local hostelry. They are shown to be close to each other, both physically and emotionally.

pp. 145–56

In the trenches morale is low. Stephen and Weir fear that the heavy bombardment they have been under is going to break the spirit of their men. They drink whisky in Stephen's dugout, and the talk turns to women. Weir admits to being a virgin, and he in turn asks Stephen about whether he has ever made love to a woman. Stephen tells him about Isabelle. As they talk a bomb explodes nearby and Stephen runs to see who is hurt. He finds a man called Douglas and holds him, reassuring him that he won't die. Another bomb explodes, sending Stephen hurtling off the ground, but he lands unharmed. One of the men carrying Douglas has been killed and Douglas is left lying on the ground.

pp. 157–66

It is now Stephen's company's turn to go on leave. It gives Stephen time to reflect on his life. We learn that after Isabelle left him he had a brief affair with a girl called Mathilde, in Paris. When war broke out he returned to London to enlist as a British soldier, rather than French, although he feels no real sense of belonging to any one country. While on leave he talks to Gray, his commanding officer, about the tunnellers, about Weir and about his need to love his men more.

pp. 167–84

Gray orders Stephen, when back in the trenches, to give armed back-up to the tunnellers as they do their work, just in case the Germans break through the often very thin walls that divide the two sides. No sooner have the men — including Jack

and Stephen — descended into the main tunnel than the Germans break through and a fight erupts. Stephen is wounded. He is dragged back to the surface but is left unaided as more serious casualties from the heavy bombardment are tended to. Stephen is close to death. Jack looks for Stephen and eventually finds him among the rotting corpses. Weir, concerned for Stephen's life, begins to panic, and resolves to kill himself if Stephen is dead.

pp. 185–93

But Stephen lives, and is taken to hospital. He watches the others on his ward trying to cope with their terrible injuries. Gray visits him and says he could accept promotion, which would mean a desk job back at HQ. Gray tells him that new orders mean that Stephen and his men will be sent to Auchonvillers where another front is opening up.

pp. 194–207

Back in the trenches Weir and Stephen discuss what they might do on leave, and Stephen says he has a surprise waiting for his friend. Weir suspects this might involve Stephen paying for him to have sex with a prostitute. Weir is scared of the prospect. In this very emotional section of the book we see Jack struggling to decide whether to read another letter from his wife, fearful that it might be bad news about their son. Stephen and Weir go to a farmhouse where they pay a mother and a daughter for sex. However, neither men can muster any enthusiasm for either woman, and they leave unfulfilled.

pp. 208–40

Jack reads his letter and learns that his son is dead. He is devastated.

Preparations for the Battle of the Somme are underway. The bombardment before the battle is seemingly unending. Stephen takes his men to the front line and Weir tells him that an enormous mine has been planted to go off just before the infantry attack. When the attack is postponed for two days Gray tells Stephen that the German barbed wire has not been cut. It is devastating news because it means that the battle will be bloody and prolonged.

Jack writes to his wife saying how thankful they must be for their son's life. They must trust in God, he tells her. Very few of the men can sleep the night before the attack. At 7.20 a.m. the mine explodes and ten minutes later the British attack. They are killed in their thousands, but Stephen manages to find protection in a deserted German trench. Jack and Shaw watch the battle from a safe place; the padre, Horrocks, joins them. After watching wave after wave of British soldiers being killed Horrocks throws away his cross, and Jack feels his own faith dying.

Stephen runs for his life and ends up in the River Ancre, swimming with German prisoners. He is rescued by a private British soldier. He tries to get back to the Front but is wounded. He wakes to find Tyson, one of Jack's friends, dressing his wounds. We learn that nearly all of Stephen's battalion has been killed. In a striking passage Weir finds Stephen in his shell-hole; it is as if the dead have become resurrected, and all the two men can do, in the face of all this suffering, is to tell each other to hold on.

Part Three: London 1978

pp. 243–78

The focus changes again, this time to London in 1978. Elizabeth Benson is 38 and has just returned from a business trip in Germany. She is a self-confident and independent woman with a good social life. One day, at her mother's house, she sees a photograph of herself when she was three years old. This starts her thinking about her past and in particular about her grandfather, about whom she knows very little. She talks to friends at work about the First World War, but they prefer not to discuss the period: it is too depressing.

Elizabeth is in a relationship with a married man (named Robert). He works for the EEC (now EU) in Brussels, and Elizabeth decides to visit him and, en route, visit the war graves of northern Europe. She stays in a hotel in Arras. The next day she travels to Albert and visits the memorial there. Here, after talking to the caretaker, she is overwhelmed to discover that the names which seem to cover every inch of the gigantic monument are for those who were missing in action.

She spends some time with Robert but, after suggesting that they marry, she begins to realise that he won't leave his wife and daughter; indeed, Robert thinks that she should leave him so that she can meet someone who can give her the family she obviously wants. But for Elizabeth he is missing the point: she loves him, and if she is going to have children then she wants Robert to be the father.

Back in England Elizabeth visits her mother again and finds some items that have the name of her grandfather, Stephen Wraysford, on them. She asks her mother (Françoise) about him and she seems vague, replying that he would have loved Elizabeth a great deal had he lived. Elizabeth takes a notebook (which seems to be written in a private language) to Irene's house (a work colleague) because her husband, Bob, is a linguist and knows a lot about cracking codes. The section ends with Elizabeth going on a date with Stuart, a man for whom she feels nothing but affection tinged with irritation.

Part Four: France 1917

pp. 281–98

We are back in France, and Stephen has been promoted to company commander, and Gray has been promoted to battalion commander. Weir is also back on the scene, but most of the men are new to Stephen. Weir, however, is not in good

shape: he is drinking more, and his nerves are even more frayed than before. To some extent this can be explained by his disillusion with his family: on a trip back to England he was unable to communicate how terrible the war was; worse, they did not seem interested.

Weir's feelings become evident one evening when he gets drunk with Stephen and a young subaltern named Ellis. Stephen tells Weir's fortune, much to Ellis's horror, and Weir goes on to express just how much contempt he has for those left at home. Stephen admits that he is fighting only for the memory of the dead. Ellis is alone in claiming that the war is a just cause: his patriotism stands out as being at odds with the other characters' sentiments. This scepticism pervades this section of the book. Jack writes a letter to his wife suggesting that the loss of their son has seriously affected his faith. He is questioning the meaning of life itself.

pp. 299–336

A German mine explodes and Weir and Stephen decide to go underground to investigate the damage to the British tunnels. They take a canary with them to check for gas. The tunnel has collapsed and the tunnellers, they believe, are dead. In another collapse of the tunnel Weir breaks his arm, and Stephen has to try to capture the canary that has escaped: in doing so he has to overcome his fear of birds.

Stephen and Ellis are allowed to go on leave to Amiens. Stephen has reservations about returning to the city where he first met Isabelle and when he is there he finds it difficult to relax. One evening, by chance, he meets Isabelle's sister, Jeanne. She tells him of Isabelle's life after leaving Stephen: of how she had, on her father's insistence, returned to Azaire. But the outbreak of war had meant that Azaire, like many of the men in the town, were taken away by the Germans, never to return. During the occupation of the town Isabelle was injured. We also learn that Lisette is married. Stephen asks Jeanne to tell Isabelle that he would like to meet her again.

Isabelle agrees to meet Stephen the next evening, and it is then that he learns of the extent of her injury: she has been scarred on one side of her face, and Stephen finds it difficult to reconcile his image of her as she was with how she is now. She tells him of her life since leaving him: her returning to Azaire's home, as well as her love affair with Max, a German soldier. She also tells him that she did receive the letter that he wrote to her from the Somme and she realised, with some pain, that Max was also in the same battle. But she does not tell him of their daughter. The initial awkwardness between them has lessened, and Stephen leaves her for the last time, wishing her well for the future.

pp. 337–52

Emotionally, Stephen is at a low point, and his commanding officer, Colonel Gray, insists that he takes some rest and spends some time working away from the front as an interpreter. The grim atmosphere continues with Jack burying Shaw, one of his closest friends, and then proceeding, in turn, to get drunk at a local *estaminet*, and then to feel guilty for enjoying himself when his friend is dead.

The characters' lives are changing all the time: Stephen receives a letter from Jeanne telling him that Isabelle is living in Munich because Max is seriously wounded. Because of her involvement with the enemy, Isabelle is now alienated from French society. Death and despair are everywhere, and no more so than in No Man's Land. Several men, including Weir and Stephen, go into this area to try to rescue some bodies that have lain there for weeks. It is a grim experience for them all, but Brennan sees the fact that he is able to rescue the body of his brother — headless and legless — as something positive: at least he knows that he will be buried with dignity.

pp. 353–81

Stephen takes the leave that Gray insisted on and goes to England. He takes a train to Burnham Market in Norfolk. He books into a small hotel and, when walking in the countryside, experiences an **epiphany**: he realises that nature is profoundly beautiful, and that he belongs to it. He also accepts the need for love and, in a fore-shadowing of the final scenes in war-torn France, of forgiveness.

This feeling remains with him as he returns to France. Once there he meets with Jeanne again and, over a meal, they talk about many things. Stephen admits to being exhausted by the war and of dreading being back in the trenches. There are moments of intimacy and affection between them, a suggestion of what might develop if the war does not intervene.

Stephen is right to be wary of a return to action. At Messines he reveals himself to be in a very fragile state of mind: he argues with Weir, and the attack that his men launch, although initially successful, begins to go wrong when there is no support provided. Many have died, including Ellis, and the sense of futility permeates the atmosphere.

pp. 382–90

At last Stephen's desk job begins, and his first task is to write to Ellis's mother informing her of his death. Writing such letters, although commonplace, now fills him with despair: he wonders about the reaction it will generate, the sadness that will come from it. He cannot think about it for very long and tries to dismiss it from his mind.

This inner turmoil is contrasted with the physical horrors of the trenches as Jack and his tunnellers prepare to attack the Messines Ridge. But it is at this moment that Weir is killed by a sniper's bullet. It is a random act of opportunism. Stephen hears of the news just before the Battle of Messines Ridge and he feels a mixture of emotions for his former friend: there is guilt because he did not leave him on good terms, but there is also affection as Stephen admits to himself that he did love him.

He finds that he does not have time to dwell on Weir's death, however, because Gray orders him to meet with some French officers to discuss the extent of a mutiny reported in the French trenches. The only hope for Stephen lies with Jeanne, and he continues to see her whenever he is allowed leave.

Part Five: London 1978

pp. 393–422

Elizabeth's pursuit of Stephen continues. She visits his regiment's headquarters and charms the officer there to allow her to have more information. She discovers that Gray is still alive and decides to telephone him. The conversation is awkward, but he does remember her grandfather, although the picture he paints is not entirely flattering. Gray's wife puts Elizabeth on to Brennan. She locates him in the Star and Garter Home in Southend. He resembles a little bird, perched on a stool. He is a pitiful character who obviously suffered post-traumatic stress disorder (or shell shock), which has lasted all his life. Elizabeth can make out very little of what he says, but the fact that she can physically connect with this man, by holding his hand, in some way brings her closer to her grandfather.

Elizabeth's relationship with Robert is still strained: he continues to contemplate leaving his wife. Elizabeth's mother tells her that she has found more documents written by Stephen; she collects them but is distracted by the arrival — at her invitation — of Stuart for dinner. She had completely forgotten about this and throws together an impromptu meal, over which he proposes to her. She promises to think about it, but has no intention of accepting.

Elizabeth discovers she is pregnant and she decides to keep the baby. She tells Robert who, although initially unsure, promises to support her. This section closes with the news that Stephen's notebooks have been 'cracked' by Irene's husband. Holding two pages in her 'shaking hand' Elizabeth comes as close as she ever has to her grandfather. The past is alive once again.

Part Six: France 1918

pp. 425–64

We rejoin Stephen in France. Stephen seems inured to further shock, and even the news that he is going to be part of the 'final push' does not faze him: he feels emotionally dead. The one ray of hope is his continuing relationship with Jeanne, and he visits her in Rouen before rejoining his company. His relationship with Jeanne continues, growing increasingly more intimate. However, when he accidentally enters her room when she is undressing he is unable to make love to her, and instead holds on to her, weeping, and crying out her sister's name.

On returning to the Front Stephen decides to inspect a tunnel. Almost immediately there is an explosion and Stephen hurts his arm, but it is not serious. Initially he thinks that he is the only man underground, but he soon hears somebody else moving close by. He finds Jack Firebrace. Another bomb explodes trapping both men underground. Jack's legs, which were trapped beneath debris, are released by Stephen, but he is too injured to walk. Stephen has to carry Jack back down the tunnel. They cannot find a way out and so are forced to talk to each other. Jack talks about the loss of his son, and Stephen talks about Isabelle. Jack does not believe that he will get out of the tunnel alive and Stephen promises that he will have Jack's children for him. They both continue to search for a way out, but they become increasingly exhausted. Eventually Stephen finds some sandbags and Jack explains that this could mean that there are explosives nearby. He is right: Stephen finds a chamber filled with explosives, but Jack explains that if they are all detonated then it will blow them up as well. Over a period of days, Stephen laboriously moves enough boxes of explosives out of the way so that he can detonate the remaining boxes in the hope that it will blast a hole in the tunnel wall, which will allow him to escape. He detonates the explosives.

pp. 464–85

Three Germans — Levi (a doctor), Lamm and Kroger — are rocked by the explosion, and they are sent down the tunnel to see if their colleagues (including Levi's brother) have been injured. They reach some debris that stops them advancing and, after sustained attempts to clear the blockage, they also decide to use a small charge to blow a way through the rubble. Stephen and Jack hear this and it gives them some hope of rescue. But Jack is weakening all the time, and Stephen holds him, talking to him about Isabelle.

Levi, Lamm and Kroger discover the body of Levi's brother. They continue to dig, albeit reluctantly, to discover if there are any more bodies that need to be buried. Jack admits to Stephen that he does not want to live any more, and passes away. Stephen is alone, and all he can do is tap on the wall with his knife, hoping to be heard. He is lucky: Levi hears the sound and the Germans work towards him. Kroger points out that they may be rescuing the men who murdered Levi's brother, but a strong moral purpose is driving the young doctor onwards. Another small charge is exploded, and they are now very close to Stephen.

In contrast with Stephen's behaviour in the past, he now seems determined to live: he thinks of Jeanne and the world outside, and this sustains him. Eventually Levi enters the small room that has held Stephen. Stephen's initial response is to attack people he sees as the enemy, but his actions are the opposite of this, and he hugs Levi, sobbing like a young child.

When they get above ground again it is clear that the war is all but over for the Germans: the British troops have advanced deep into their territory. The men decide to bury Joseph Levi in the same grave as Jack Firebrace: it is a symbolic gesture, but not the only one because Stephen and Levi exchange tokens of peace and promise

to keep in touch with each other after the war. Stephen leaves to find his regiment, exhausted but thoroughly alive.

Part Seven: England 1979

pp. 489–503

Elizabeth has finished reading Stephen's notebooks. She now knows about his being trapped underground, and of how he promised Jack that he would have his children for him. Her thoughts are with her own child, and she is dreading telling her mother that she is pregnant. She also wants to ask her about the dates she has read about: Jeanne's date of birth and marriage do not tie in with her mother's date of birth.

Over dinner Elizabeth tells her mother that she is expecting a baby and, much to Elizabeth's surprise, her mother takes it very well. She admits that she cannot be too judgemental because her own parents were unmarried when she was born. She goes on to explain that she is not Jeanne's daughter but Isabelle's, and that she was sent to live with Jeanne and Stephen in 1919 after Isabelle had died of influenza. After the war, she says, Stephen, Jeanne and herself settled in Norfolk, but her father was deeply traumatised by the war and did not speak for two years. He died at the age of 48. He never knew that she was his real daughter and always thought that he was her stepfather. Jeanne had nursed him right to the end, and they were both very fond of each other. Françoise regretted that Stephen never lived to see Elizabeth.

Elizabeth and Robert rent a cottage in the countryside to have the baby. Soon, Elizabeth goes into labour and the baby is born before the doctor can come; when she does arrive she dismisses Robert to the garden, and he walks through some fallen conkers, kicking them in joy, overwhelmed with life.

With this birth the book ends on a note of hope, but it also ends looking back at a reconciled past, with birdsong sounding in the air and the knowledge that the promise that Stephen made to Jack — that he would have a John for him — has been kept with the naming of Elizabeth's first son by the same name. The past, present and future have become joined, for now at least.

Characters

Stephen Wraysford

Stephen Wraysford is not a conventional hero: we do not always sympathise with his position, nor do we understand his actions. Indeed, Faulks seems to be constantly challenging us to reconsider how a hero should behave, and this is as true in the domestic sphere as it is on the battlefield.

Stephen's father worked for the Post Office in Lincolnshire; his mother worked in a factory; in many ways he comes from a broken home ('They were not married, and when she became pregnant he disappeared. I never met him.'). His mother abandoned him to his grandfather, a farm labourer, and she eventually became a maid in a large house. His grandfather taught Stephen how to fish, as well as how to steal and fight. When he was imprisoned for a small crime Stephen was taken into care. In what reads like a premonition of regimental dinners, Stephen describes his time in the home as cold and intimidating:

> ...the feel of the uniform against the skin. I remember the big room with a ceiling that was so high it was almost lost to view and the long tables we ate from...I'd never seen so many people in one place before and it seemed to me each one of us was diminished by it. I had feelings of panic when we sat there, as though we were all being reduced to numbers, to ranks of nameless people who were not valued in the eyes of another individual.

He is an intense and rather distant young man: we read that Isabelle is frightened of his 'dark face and its staring brown eyes, and his swift impetuous movements'. This tendency to act without thinking can be seen as an attractive quality at times, but it is also potentially very dangerous. Stephen's 'confidence in himself was not checked by judgement; he followed where nothing more than instinct took him, and relied on some reflexive wariness to help'. In the trenches such behaviour could prove fatal, both to oneself and the men who serve under you.

Such rebelliousness is the result of his upbringing. When he was placed in an institution he believes he lost his individuality. It was here that he developed his phobia about birds when he tried to prove himself to others by touching a dead crow: '"I went up and stroked one to show I was not afraid. It had maggots under its wings and drooling, milky eyes." He shuddered.' Birds, for many the **symbol** of beauty and hope, are for Stephen symbolic of corrupted life and of death. They also signify for Stephen something primeval, something 'cruel, prehistoric'.

Vaughan read about Stephen and soon became his guardian. They did not, however, have a close emotional relationship and, perhaps as a result, Stephen has been able to form very few — if any — lasting ties with other people.

It could be argued that Stephen Wraysford changes a great deal over the course of the novel, and that each of these changes is caused by external influences: his childhood, his affair with Isabelle, his experiences in the trenches, his ability to embrace Levi at the end: through these Faulks shows how our environment shapes us.

Stephen experiences an emotional 'epiphany' when he meets Isabelle: the intensity of his experiences with this older woman perhaps emphasises both his youth and his naivety. To some extent this is not surprising, but what does surprise the reader is Isabelle's emotional response. There is an understood sense that their relationship is always going to be short-lived: indeed, what we are asked to contemplate

is the veracity of their feelings for each other. It could be that, like the touching of the crow, Stephen's affair with Isabelle is another attempt to prove himself.

Responsibility is forced on Stephen in a rapid sequence of events: he moves to France, begins an affair, breaks up a marriage, resigns from his job and begins living with a woman. He also becomes a father, although he does not learn of this. At the beginning of the novel Stephen is comparatively young (he is 20, nine years younger than Isabelle) and this, to some extent, might also explain his impetuous behaviour which later, in the trenches, turns to recklessness.

He celebrates his twenty-first birthday in Grenoble. This is significant for Stephen because it is the day he becomes a man in his own right: he leaves his employment and, at the same time, writes to Vaughan to thank him for his 'guardianship', which is now over. Soon after they settle in St-Rémy-de-Provence. It is autumn, a fitting season for the beginning of a bleak time for both Stephen and Isabelle. Stephen gets a job as an assistant to a furniture maker. He remains something of an outsider: 'he could see they thought him curious and he tried not to outstay his welcome'. This inability to be intimate with others extends to Stephen's relationship with Isabelle: Faulks remarks that he 'found the closeness of Isabelle's unconscious body made him feel uneasy, and he often took a blanket to the sofa in the living room' (p. 108). Over time this fear of intimacy recedes; indeed, on three different occasions — when he holds Douglas, Weir and Jack — Stephen embraces another person to comfort and reassure them.

As he and Isabelle move apart he begins to draw more heavily on the routine of everyday life: such patterns give meaning, however superficial, even in times of conflict. Even after she has left him he still 'swore and spat at the snagging teeth of the saw as the blade caught in the grainy timber…He talked and told jokes with the men and showed no sign that anything had changed' (p. 117).

Time moves on, seemingly indifferent to our concerns. Stephen discovers that the tragedy of much of life is that he has 'no choice but to continue with what he had begun'. Life is remorseless, even when one feels oneself growing 'cold'. Once Isabelle leaves him Stephen is, again, abandoned and alone. He is rejected by someone he has formed a strong attachment to, but we are left in no doubt that their relationship is doomed once the initial surge of emotion is spent. To some extent Stephen's relationship with Isabelle is asking us to reappraise what constitutes a conventionally 'romantic' relationship, and to question its value in the face of destructive forces. This rejection by Isabelle prepares Stephen for the often overwhelming indifference of the trenches; indeed, it is made clear that he, like many men, join up not to fight a cause but to gain a sense of order, to establish a pattern in an otherwise shapeless world. This desire for structure — and *sense* — is made manifest in many different ways: from the military rules, routines and orders, to the 'voodoo' that Stephen practises.

Stephen's career in the army is uneven. He is seen by Sergeant Adams as 'a law unto himself' (p. 132), to his friend Michael Weir he is 'a cold bastard' (p. 149);

Brennan later tells his granddaughter, Elizabeth, that 'we all thought he was mad'. The war ages him, turning him prematurely grey. He reaches the rank of lieutenant (in charge of an infantry platoon). He loses a great deal and to some extent he becomes fearless, but he also gains a degree of humanity that will shape him and his future, as well as how people view him. This is seen when the dying Douglas is comforted by Stephen, and when he comforts Jack Firebrace and Michael Weir. These moments of kindness do not go unnoticed; indeed, when Elizabeth listens to Brennan, it is the fact that 'he had comforted a dying man' that remains in her mind.

When Stephen and Isabelle meet again he is afraid. His first thoughts are: 'this is fear…this is what makes men cower in shellholes or shoot themselves' (p. 327). He is shocked but, in a striking intersection of the personal and the public, he admits to himself that what appalled him was 'the sense of gross intimacy. Through her skin and blood he had found things no exploding metal should have followed' (p. 330). The war has found its way into every crevice of his life, and although the old emotions he felt for her linger, they inevitably lack the intensity of his prewar youth.

Through force of circumstances Stephen spends more time in the company of Isabelle's sister, Jeanne. It is on a visit to see her, after he has said goodbye to Isabelle for the final time, that 'he felt the last presence of Isabelle leave him'. Faulks makes an important distinction here when he writes that this loss is not a process of 'going into false oblivion, as she had the first time, but into simple absence' (p. 367). At the same time he notices Jeanne as a person in her own right: her smile lights up her face, 'not with blood as Isabelle's might have done, but with an inner light that made it shine…her whole face…changed into something forgiving and serene' (p. 367). They are drawn together and he visits her again before he returns to the trenches. She encourages him to be strong; she feels he is lucky, and that he will survive. But at the end of Part Four we read that he is almost devoid of his humanity: 'he managed only to exist. His life became grey and thin…it was filled with quietness' (p. 390). Ironically, Stephen seems to have been transformed into an officer well equipped to deal with the coming horror: he cares for his men, but is desensitised to his own fate. It is only when he is at the point of death that he sees how precious life is.

Stephen is afraid of dying, and this surprises him. When he faces death with Jack he decides that, should the moment arrive, he will take his own life because at least he will have control over his own fate. Faulks writes that 'there was a perverse appeal in the thought that he would complete what no enemy had managed'. But such a thought is not as strong as the desire to live. In contrast to Jack, Stephen has not seen the very foundations of his life disintegrate: to some extent, his rootless existence has inured him to caring very deeply about attachments. However, there is no doubt that the episode with Jack changes him profoundly, and his behaviour towards Levi, to a great extent, transcends the temporal and physical setting of the novel by looking ahead to the next world conflict. At the end of the war Stephen

has learned to overcome his hatred of Germans and, in a symbolic gesture, embraces Levi ('weeping at the bitter strangeness of their human lives'), the man indirectly responsible for Jack's death (and the man whose brother Stephen has killed). The final 're-birth' of Stephen shapes him forever. His farewell handshake with Levi, a doctor who, because of the conflict, had been forced to kill rather than save, makes a significant impression on him: 'of all the flesh he had seen and touched, it was this doctor's hand that had signalled his deliverance' (p. 485).

Stephen married Jeanne and they lived in England. Whether or not he loved her is debatable: Elizabeth thinks to herself that his descriptions of her were 'not the language of passion' (p. 491). After the war Stephen did not talk for two years. When Elizabeth's mother was ten years old, he stood up and, after breakfast, announced that they were going to the theatre in London that evening. The change was sudden and unexplained. But even with his returned 'voice' Stephen did not talk about the war, nor did he ever recover ('like a lot of men of that generation', p. 494). He died at the age of 48, two years before Elizabeth was born. His wife, Jeanne, 'the heroine of the story', lives long enough to see her granddaughter born.

Faulks is constantly asking us to consider to what extent fate plays a part in each of his characters' lives. He is, to some extent, positing a determinist philosophy: namely, that our actions have immediate consequences but, as with Weir's death, life has a randomness that cannot be accounted for or explained. Stephen understands this, and this provides him with a degree of indifference that is misconstrued by some as bravery, by others as recklessness. What is true is that he chose to live, and Jack chose to die.

Isabelle Azaire

Isabelle Azaire (neé Fourmentier) was born near Rouen, the youngest of five girls (p. 34). Like Stephen she did not have a conventionally happy relationship with her parents; indeed, Faulks tells us that she 'had disappointed her father by not being the son he had wanted' (p. 34). Father figures in the novel are often disappointing or damaging, and Isabelle's is no exception: he exerts a 'remote tyranny' over his daughters when he takes an interest in their development, but for the most part he is indifferent to this female household. As with Azaire, all is not well in the marital bed: her father 'showed no interest in' Isabelle's mother, with the result that she spends a great deal of time on her appearance in the hope that she will attract some interest from other men. She, too, is described as being indolent and manipulative. To some extent this interest in fashion is shared by her youngest daughter, as is the need to be appreciated by men.

When her first male acquaintance, a young infantry officer called Jean Destournel, began to court her she responded positively, but 'didn't care whether he married her or not, but when he said he would not see her again she felt the simple agony of bereavement, like a child whose only source of love has gone' (p. 37). In a foreshadowing of her later scarring, Faulks describes this loss as being 'like a wound on which the skin would not thicken'. Tellingly, this vulnerability is always exposed, always likely to be opened, and we are left wondering if her passion for Stephen is, in some way, an attempt to revisit her lost, unrequited first 'affair'.

She meets René Azaire, a widower with two young children, when she is 23. Love is not mentioned at any time in their relationship (in fact he would have been 'frightened to have aroused such an unnecessary emotion' in her): René and her father 'adroitly' sell the relationship to her. It is viewed by the men as a business proposal, but Isabelle sees the marriage as an opportunity to free herself of her parents, as well as to have her own family. To begin with at least she is an 'affectionate and dutiful wife to her husband'. However, René views sex as a means for producing children, which are in turn 'an important proof of his standing in society': there is no real intimacy between them and each month, as her period arrives, they grow further apart. She never reconciles 'this secret thing that promised new life and liberation' with 'the colour of pain': each period becomes a mark of failure, of rebuke, and red, the colour of passion and death, also becomes the symbol of a lack of life, of love not bodied forth. By the time Stephen arrives Isabelle's life has become, in every sense, sterile: she has not made love with her husband for a year and René begins to blame her for the loss of passion ('He said I castrated him,' she confesses to Stephen on p. 76).

Isabelle Azaire is attractive but not conventionally 'beautiful' (p. 28). We are told that although 'everything was feminine about her face, her nose was slightly larger than fashion prescribed; her hair had more different shades of brown and gold and red than most women would have wanted. For all her lightness of her face, its obvious strength of character overpowered conventional prettiness'. She has 'strawberry-chestnut hair, caught and held up off her face' (pp. 6–7). She wears 'a white lace blouse with a dark red stone at the throat', perhaps foreshadowing the injury that will later disfigure her. She has a natural poise: her voice is 'cool and low' (p. 9). Stephen views her as 'magnificent' in her dismissive treatment of Bérard.

In his notebook Stephen uses the word 'pulse' as code for Isabelle. He feels that there was 'a keener physical life than she was actually living', and of course he wants to discover if this impression is correct. Faulks writes (p. 22):

> It seemed to him to be sufficiently cryptic, yet also to suggest something of his suspicion that she was animated by a different kind of rhythm from that which beat in her husband's blood. It also referred to an unusual aspect of her physical presence. No one could have been more proper in their dress and toilet than Madame Azaire. She spent long parts of the day bathing or changing her clothes; she carried a light scent of rose soap or perfume when she brushed past him in the passageways. Her clothes were more fashionable than those of other women in the town yet revealed less. She carried herself modestly when she sat or stood; she slid into chairs with her feet close together so that beneath the

folds of her skirts her knees too must have been almost touching. When she rose again it was without any leverage from her hands or arms but with a sponta-neous upward movement of grace and propriety. Her white hands seemed barely to touch the cutlery when they ate at the family dinner table and her lips left no trace of their presence on the wine glass.

But behind this façade lies great passion. Such scrutiny tells us as much about Stephen's interest in Madame Azaire as it does about Isabelle herself: in that sense it has a dual narrative purpose. It also reveals a great deal about the society Madame Azaire lives in. Faulks is unambiguous in presenting her as essentially a morally good character: she has passion, as well as a sense of social obligation, which is at odds with the spirit of the times: this is a woman who is described as 'gentle…young, vital…beautiful, interesting' (pp. 36–37), a woman transported by the chance sound of music coming from a window, one who unquestioningly cares for another man's children, and who is able to act altruistically by taking food to Lucien Lebrun and the striking dyers' families (pp. 31–33).

Isabelle's passion eventually overwhelms her: the emotions that she has tried to repress are impossible to contain once Stephen has revealed his feelings for her. The same is true for him but, importantly, Faulks hints at the darker side of male sexuality when he writes that 'the force that drove through him could not be stopped. The part of his mind that remained calm accepted this; if the necessity could not be denied, then the question was only whether it could be achieved with her consent' (p. 58). Does this mean that he would have raped her if she had rejected him? It is hypothetical because we quickly learn that, in a mixture of feelings, which combine the dominant and the submissive, she 'wanted to comfort him but also to be taken by him, to be used by him. Currents of desire and excitement that she had not known or thought about for years now flooded in her. She wanted him to bring alive what she had buried, and to demean, destroy, her fabricated self' (p. 58).

When they make love the narrative perspective is closer to Isabelle than Stephen. It is her emotions that we are forced to consider in detail, her release that seems the most profound: 'I am at last what I am, she thought; I was born for this. Fragments of childish longings, of afternoon urges suppressed in the routine of her parents' house, flashed across her mind; she felt at last connections forged between the rage of her desire and a particular attentive recognition of herself, the little Fourmentier girl' (p. 60).

The love affair she has with Stephen is necessary and intense, but it is not, for Isabelle, the beginning of the life-long love affair that Stephen dreamt of having with her. The confrontation between her, René and Stephen forces her to suddenly assess herself, and she surprises herself: 'I won't listen to either of you. Why should I? How do I know that you love me Stephen? How can I tell…And you, René, why should I trust you when you have given me so little reason even to like you?' That she has to choose one tells us something about the position of women at the time, and one should compare and contrast Isabelle's situation with Elizabeth's in England in the 1970s.

From Amiens they travel south towards Soissons and Reims. The journey is paved with irony: Isabelle notices the rivers, including 'Verdun — a flat, unargued path through the lowlands of her native country', which once again links the domestic dispute of the narrative to the imminent conflict of the coming war.

She settles with Stephen in southern France, but cannot help comparing — often unfavourably — the relatively impoverished life she is forced to lead: the clothes and the food are poorer than those she is used to ('compared to the bourgeois opulence of the boulevard du Cange, the room was stark', p. 107) but in time the sense of loss she has felt is replaced by her pregnancy. To begin with she does not tell Stephen. She views her child as a young man, similar to all the others, but again with added (and unconscious) poignancy. They exist 'out there…strong, smiling…working on the land. They never knew each other, never met, never considered any kinship or allegiance they might have to each other or to the country they lived in, because such things existed only in time of war' (p. 110).

As her emotions change so does her attitude to Stephen: 'the excesses of their brazen love affair seemed to belong to a different season'. Like many who embark on a love affair she realises that much of the thrill is a result of its illicit nature: 'without the stimulus of fear and prohibition, her desire had slackened' (p. 111). As they become less intimate it becomes easier for Isabelle to conceal her pregnancy from him ('some new-found modesty meant that he never had a chance to examine her properly without her clothes', p. 116).

They drift apart, slowly, and she eventually decides to return to her sister, Jeanne, in Rouen. Isabelle leaves Stephen because 'she felt she could save her soul. She had gone home because she was frightened of the future and felt sure a natural order could yet be resumed'. She writes him a note, but decides to destroy it, leaving him with only silence and absence. He remains ignorant of her pregnancy. We learn, later on in the novel, that Azaire is persuaded to take Isabelle back. At the outbreak of the war her husband, like most of the men in the town, is deported to Germany.

When they meet again, in 1917, Isabelle and Stephen are much changed, both physically and psychologically: he 'beyond recognition…His hair was shot with grey…he was badly shaved…His eyes had always been dark, but now they seemed shrunk. There was no light in them…He seemed a man removed to some new existence where he was dug in and fortified by his lack of natural feeling or response' (p. 334–35); 'the left side of [Isabelle's] face was disfigured by a long indentation that ran from the corner of her ear, along the jaw, whose natural line seemed broken, then down her neck and disappeared beneath the high collar of her dress' (p. 328). She tells Stephen that she was injured by a shell in the apartment she had moved to after René's departure. She also tells him that a young Prussian soldier, Max, had looked after her and that she had fallen in love with him. She tells Stephen of this, but she does not

tell him of their daughter: to do so would have made things more complicated between them. That child — Françoise — goes on to become Elizabeth's mother. For Isabelle, Max is a man 'of great courtesy…of imagination, stability and humour. For the first time in her life she felt she had met someone with whom she could be happy under any circumstances' (p. 333). Compared to her relationship with Stephen it was 'muted' but not 'shallow'. He presented her with a chance to redeem her life.

Before she leaves Stephen for the final time she allows him to touch the scar, and she wonders if he can feel 'the quality of her flesh'. The war has, both literally and figuratively, desensitised him, callousing both his hands and soul. She is, for the last time, overcome with desire for him, and as he traces her scar it feels, to her, as if his fingers 'were opening the flesh between her legs'. He leaves her, though, and there is a sense of finality about his departure: they will not see each other again.

Isabelle stays with Max, nursing him through his injury, but because he is German she becomes an outcast from the local community. After the war she moves to Germany with him, but succumbs to influenza, like millions of others in Europe after the First World War. Her daughter is sent to live with Jeanne in 1919, when she is seven years old. Isabelle's life ends not in glory but in sadness, just like Stephen. Although she is not a victim of the war in a conventional sense Faulks seems to be saying that war damages everyone it comes into contact with, even those who, outwardly at least, 'survive' it.

To some extent both Isabelle and Stephen seem trapped by their gender. Stephen is condemned to war — the ultimate of 'masculine' pursuits — and Isabelle is condemned to being a social pariah, partly because of her affair but mainly because she is having a relationship with a German. Our fates are dependent on many things, but time and gender contribute significantly to how we are able to live.

Jack Firebrace

Our first encounter with Jack is striking: 'Jack Firebrace lay forty-five feet underground with several hundred thousand tons of France above his face' (p. 121).

The break with the previous section seems total: what crises we have read about up to this point have been essentially domestic; now we are in France six years later, in the middle of the war, and we suspect that the problems we are about to read about are going to be more extreme in every way. War transforms not only the present but the past. We quickly learn that Jack is underground for a reason: he is digging a tunnel to listen for German activity, as well as to plant huge mines. Tellingly, in an overt piece of symbolism, he is moved about the place on 'a wooden cross': is Faulks signalling to us that this character is not only good, but that he even has Christ-like qualities? Time will tell.

If he is sent from heaven he is, ironically, seemingly at home in a subterranean hell: 'he had lost track of how long he had been underground' Faulks writes, but we later read that he had been involved in 'the construction of the Central Line' (something that will link him with Elizabeth Benson when we meet her for the first time). He is 38 years old, with 'a big, square…flat, guileless face' and a good sense of humour. He is something of a showman, enjoying singing, conjuring tricks and drawing. He joined up because he had no work to do in London. He told his wife, Margaret, that the war would be over by Christmas. At the beginning of the novel his religious faith is strong: he prays regularly (indeed, when Stephen is believed to be dead Jack decides to pray for him: 'I will at least do my duty as a Christian', p. 180) but he is, like all the other men, scared of dying. Although Faulks writes that Jack is 'immune to death' (p. 125) he would sacrifice any of them to save himself: 'let them die, he prayed shamefully; let them die, but please God let me live'. His desire, above all else, is to see his son, John, but this becomes increasingly difficult over time.

All the major characters change a great deal in this novel, but none more so than Jack. His change is brought about through loss: the loss of his child, the loss of his friends, and the loss of his faith. There is a side to Jack that, to some students, seems unconvincing, and this is the 'music hall entertainer', the popular character at the heart of drunken company. We see this side of the character after his friend, Shaw, is buried. Jack proceeds to get drunk but he does so in order to forget. In a passage that is reminiscent of the earlier episode in which Jack tries, with some difficulty, to recall an image of his son, he tries to conjure up a memory of Shaw:

> …the features of his dead friend came back. Shaw had been, in this strange
> alternate life, the only person in the world to him: his handsome head with its
> level eyes, his muscular back and huge, broken-nailed fingers. Jack could almost
> feel the supple shape of Shaw's body as it had curved to accommodate him in
> the narrow, stinking dugouts where they had slept…I have made this mistake in
> my life, Jack thought: not once but twice I have loved someone more than my
> heart would bear.

There are distinct overtones of homoeroticism here: Shaw and Jack had a degree of intimacy and understanding which, although not realised sexually, has a sensuousness that goes beyond purely heterosexual friendship. When they bathe together Jack thinks to himself that 'there was a moment of friendship and relaxation such as he had barely known'. None of this lasts; its passing contributes to Jack's final ability to 'let go' of life. What is clear is that Jack certainly seems to 'need' somebody at every stage of the book: if it is not John then it is Shaw, and if not Shaw then Stephen. Indeed, he transfers his interest from Shaw — most obviously represented in his drawings of his friend — to Stephen, and again there are overtones of something other than simple friendship (p. 372):

> Jack had taken to drawing Stephen…From the moment he had pitched into his
> arms, back from the dead, Jack had been intrigued by him. Now he had made
> drawings of his large dark head from many angles and in many poses — with his
> big eyes open in incredulity…of the smile with which he chafed his own officer,
> Captain Weir.

Jack is an observer, a character who watches but does not often judge, who is known for his ability to listen ('His exceptional hearing was frequently in demand', p. 122). His drawings are possibly an attempt to restore permanence to a world of brutal transience, or at creating something beautiful in a world of ugliness. In this sense he is similar to famous war poets such as Owen and Sassoon. We watch him as he loses everything that once sustained him, just as many millions of others did before him. But what does he gain? To some extent he gains a sense of self-awareness as we are made to feel that, despite his more limited vocabulary, he is a thinking, sensitive character who is able to reveal another side to the human condition. This is seen in his letters to his wife, but it is most movingly articulated in the final moments of Jack's life, when he is buried alive with Stephen Wraysford. These two characters are connected through life and death: it is Stephen who 'saves' Jack's life by deciding not to press charges when Jack was asleep on duty; Jack returns this 'favour' when he finds Stephen, almost at the point of death, dumped with corpses after a German attack. Their interaction is also the inter-action of the middle and lower classes, and to a great extent it foreshadows the greater ease of communication between the classes that was one of the many legacies of the war.

Jack admits that the loss of his son, two years earlier, effectively meant the end of his own life: 'I loved that boy...My world was in his face...He was from another world, he was a blessing too great for me' (pp. 451–52) He understands the value of love, and for that he is grateful because in this world such a gift should never be taken for granted, nor should it be discarded lightly. In this he and Stephen are very similar: they have both lost what they have loved. Jack's faith was love, and that love was bound up with his son; when that died so did his faith, rendering his existence empty:

> The things on which he had based his faith had proved unstable. John's innocence, the message from a better world, had been taken from him. Any meetings he might have with Margaret and any rekindling of love he might feel would also prove illusory. Love had betrayed him, and he no longer wished to be reunited with his life. (p. 454)

Jack dies because there is nothing to live for; his world has changed utterly and all that he believed in has gone. Faulks uses this character to explore how an 'ordinary man' experiences the extraordinary. Jack's ability to reflect and change, and to some extent take the brave decision to let go of life, is an experience that many will have shared in this war and continue to live today. Jack is buried with Joseph Levi's brother, a symbolic gesture on many levels: he is returned to his natural, subter-ranean habitat, but in being buried with the enemy his grave becomes a lasting memorial to hope.

As a character Jack is most convincing when he is a colleague and a father. The passages in which he toils with others and reflects on his son's life and death are amongst the most powerful and moving in the novel. Perhaps less convincing are the passages where Jack is transformed into the 'life and soul of the party'. We see him as a morally 'upright' character who never swears and who for much of the novel is secure in his faith, and this is at odds with the entertainer who serenades the troops, or who gets drunk to forget the death of Shaw. Another possible answer could be to see this as the development of a complex character, and that Jack's unfolding personality shows the reader how he changes in response to the conditions he lives in.

Captain Michael Weir

The first encounter with Captain Michael Weir takes place immediately after the first description of Jack Firebrace: he is 'a startling figure with disarrayed hair, in plimsolls and civilian sweater'; he has 'a round, honest face with receding fair hair' (p. 149). Elsewhere, when Stephen thinks of him after his death, he is described as having a 'puzzled, open face, its chalky skin patched red with blood vessels broken up by drink'; his 'balding skull and shocked eyes' could not contain his innocence. Stephen describes him as 'a strange man, but perhaps no stranger than anyone else in the circumstances'. He is a sapper — a member of the Royal Engineers who is in charge of Jack's company of tunnellers (or 'clay kickers' as they are pejoratively referred to by Gray), itself a group of men who are looked down upon by others in the regiment as being a rather sordid and underhand necessity.

He is 32 years old and was born in Leamington Spa. The very outward ordinariness of his life — as we see when he returns to visit his parents — hides a host of uncomfortable truths: he is an alcoholic who has never had a relationship with a woman. Like Stephen he is an only child. His experiences in the trenches have made him despise the country — and the people — he is (in name at least) fighting for, but whatever he once fought for has long since gone, ground down by endless, systematic but seemingly random acts of brutality. Stephen, with his 'hocus pocus' provides him with the only meaning — or comfort — that he can rely upon.

Weir is a complex character. He is very vulnerable, as well as being, outwardly at least, resilient. Faulks writes that 'in his oblique and drunken way Weir was as passionate as Stephen' (p. 374), but what is he passionate about? He, like the men he serves with, seems to have lost contact with his background: the England that he is fighting for has ceased to have any meaning, and his anger often springs from the hypocrisy he feels lies at the core of the conflict. He is fighting for a country that does not recognise and that seems indifferent about him. This seems to be true on the personal level. When he returns home on leave he seems a stranger in his own land; indeed, the maid who answers the door of his home asks him who he is and worse, his father does not look up when he first speaks to him (p. 286).

The exchanges between Weir and his father are filled with awkwardness: he even has to apologise for staying the night, and he notices that his father does not exchange one word of greeting. Home had become defamiliarised, and as he waited

for it to return to what it once was 'nothing happened. The polished mahogany of the chest looked alien: it was hard to imagine that he had seen it before'. His old life is there in a physical sense only: 'the familiar recollection did not bring back any sense of belonging'. His mother greets him with a kiss but he eats his meal alone with water to wash it down.

His mother, in a phrase that has extra resonance given the context, is glad to see him back 'in one piece', but she does not stay up past 10 p.m.; instead she leaves the two men to talk, awkwardly, about the war. He finds it impossible to convey to his father the true horror of the war. His father, in turn, tries to calm his son down but, as ever, the only thing that will work is alcohol. The final image we have of Weir at home is redolent of him in the trenches: he is alone at night, smoking, drinking, his hand shaking with either fear or anger, or both.

When he returns to the Front his views on what was once home are bitter and direct. He says to Ellis and Stephen that he wishes 'a great bombardment would smash down along Piccadilly into Whitehall and kill the whole lot of them'. He does not spare his family either: 'I would especially like a five-day bombardment on their street...I would like to see them all walk into the enemy guns in long thin lines'. His anger never subsides.

His death surprises us because it is so sudden and unexpected. Jack — again, the witness to so much in this novel — tries to warn Weir that some of the protective sandbags are missing and that he might be seen by the enemy. His warning is too late: Weir, looking happier than usual, steps up onto a firestep to let a ration party past and is shot through the head by a German sniper. The shock is palpable: 'his body seemed for a moment unaware of what had happened...then it fell like a puppet, its limbs shooting out, and the face smashing unprotected into mud' (p. 385).

Stephen hears of the death the next day. He admits to himself that he 'had loved him'; indeed, Weir had made the war 'bearable' for Stephen because his fear 'had been a conductor for his own fear'. More tellingly, perhaps, Stephen notes that: 'in his innocent character Stephen had been able to mock the qualities he himself had lost. Weir had been braver by far than he was: he had lived with horror, he had known it every day, and by his strange stubbornness he had defeated it.' His death leaves Stephen 'more lonely than ever in his life before' because 'only Weir had been with him into the edges of reality where he had lived; only Weir had heard the noise of the sky at Thiepval' (p. 385). But like others in the book, Stephen rapidly views the death from his own perspective: he thinks of the pity of such a life, of such a brief time spent alive, and to be returned to the earth 'without knowledge of another human body'. He tries to cry for his old friend, but 'no tears would come to express his desolation or his love for poor mad Weir'. In death, as in life, Weir, like all the characters, comes to symbolise a particular aspect of the trenches: he is the innocent man, driven to recklessness by war and horror, convinced of his country's unworthiness to be defended, and taken, suddenly, and too young, by a random act of cruelty. There is no pattern to any of it and the bleakness of such a death springs from this realisation.

Perhaps because of this it seems that of all the main characters, Weir's life is the most empty of meaning. He seldom reflects on what he is experiencing with any lasting benefit; instead, he seems nihilistic in his view of life, preferring to believe in 'the runes' that Stephen conjures with underground, or to get drunk to blot out the awfulness of the war. To some extent we can understand why Weir wants to believe in 'fortune'; as Stephen says, 'it makes him feel that somebody cares about him. It's better to have a malign providence than an indifferent one' (p. 290). But Weir's death proves that whether there is a vengeful or uncaring God makes little or no difference: we die anyway, and our lives are uncertain. In the sense that he was a good soldier who made a difference to his men and the campaign, to some extent Weir's life can be read as having value; however, Faulks uses the character to show how alienated he had become from his old life (perhaps tellingly, he is more often referred to by his surname than any of the other main characters), and how war had driven him — and others — to a point that was probably incompatible with sanity. No life is entirely futile, but we are supposed to see this character as being typical of many: lonely, isolated; sustained by orders, routine and alcohol, and desperate for meaning in a meaningless universe.

Elizabeth Benson

Birdsong has two distinct narrative focuses: early twentieth-century France and modern-day England. Elizabeth is the main character in this second narrative. She is Stephen's granddaughter. She differs in many ways from Isabelle (the other main female character): she is independent, a career woman (she runs a clothing company selling couture), she is sociable and at ease with others. But there are great similarities between them as well: both are mistresses — Isabelle with Stephen and Elizabeth with Robert; both are, in very different ways, caught up in the war. Importantly, Elizabeth is also beautiful, poised and elegant (as the reference to Anouk Aimée on p. 245 makes clear); they also both have illegitimate children. The last similarity only serves to expose the many differences between the two societies: modern England seems like a different world from France in 1916, but Faulks uses Elizabeth to show how the links are real and permanent (in fact we first meet Elizabeth as she sits on a train in the Underground, thus linking her to one of the builders of the tube lines — Jack Firebrace).

Elizabeth is 38 and childless at the start of her narrative; Lindsay claims that she scares men; indeed, in this new world men are described as 'timid creatures' by the same friend, a statement that is meant to show up the changes that have taken place in 60 years. But this statement is supported, to some extent, by the male characters in this second section: her lover, Robert, seems weak and indecisive (indeed he 'pretended that Elizabeth did not exist', p. 260); in many ways he seems the opposite

of her (he seeks to 'remove the traces of his family' from her, whereas she spends much of the novel trying to restore her family). Her father, Alec, is absent, a drinker and womaniser who has no sense of responsibility towards his daughter, or Elizabeth's mother, Françoise. It is Elizabeth who instigates the search for her grandfather, Stephen, by asking her mother if there are any papers of his in the attic.

This sets off a process that leads to Stephen's story: it is she who feels 'there's a danger of losing touch with the past', and so wishes to understand it, to make sense of it herself. In getting to know Stephen she will, she feels, understand herself better. She senses something more profound waiting to be born within her: 'a larger life…something unfulfilled, something needing to be understood' (p. 254). This sense of having a life that is 'entirely frivolous' continues to haunt her and, to a great extent, explains why she seeks to make sense of her past. This modern narrative perspective, shot through as it is with self-doubt, allows the reader to reassess the passages in a different light. Elizabeth is the lens through which the reader will judge an essentially modern condition: namely, that for 'her generation there was no intensity' (p. 414). The past seems more profound, but it has seemingly disappeared, leaving only the superficial.

But the past is all around her: the train that she travels in under London has a carriage like 'a shell', it fits its tube 'like a bullet in the barrel of a gun'. We meet her in November, at the time of the sixtieth anniversary of the Armistice; furthermore, one of her designers — Erich — is Austrian, and escaped from Nazism in the mid-1930s. To some extent her relationship with Robert, as well as the inclusion of Erich, shows the reader how much Europe has changed since the two world wars: Robert works for the EEC (now EU), a symbol of greater political integration (even Elizabeth's car is Swedish, p. 272). Such details continue to build up over the course of the chapters dedicated to Elizabeth's story, and each reveal the differences and similarities between the past and present.

Elizabeth is a keen observer of life: she 'enjoyed the small physical details she noticed on her own' (p. 262), and she is also aware of how others see her, especially men. Unlike Isabelle she is able to dine alone and drink wine, make love to a strange young man (p. 255), work for herself, and she is able to seek — and find — meaning in her actions. When alone she can observe, think and understand that what links us to our pasts matters 'passionately'. It is when she first visits the graves of northern France that she undergoes an epiphany that changes her life forever: at the Albert Memorial she realises that the seemingly endless list of names cover only those who were lost in the surrounding fields. Suddenly, the sheer scale of the war hits home: '"Nobody told me." She ran her fingers with their red-painted nails back through her thick dark hair. "My God, nobody told me"' (p. 264). She goes on to spend some time with Robert and she asks him when they can marry, and he says he can't leave his wife, Jane, and his ten-year-old daughter, Anne. We are left in no doubt that she loves him, but that they are in an impossibly compromised situation.

She then returns to England to search through the trunks in her mother's attic. She is looking for something, possibly herself, and to some extent she needs to be convinced that her life has its own merits because, as Faulks writes, 'it was difficult to see her own life as the pinnacle of previous generations' sacrifices' (p. 271). It is here that she discovers Stephen's notebooks. She decides to take them to Irene (her work colleague) and Bob (Irene's husband).

A trail of enquiry begins, which leads to Elizabeth telephoning Gray and visiting Brennan. Gray forces her to question whether the quest she is pursuing is really worthwhile ('what was it all for?…Understand more about herself?…Perhaps it was just a whim…'). Brennan seems even less promising: in another reference to birds Brennan is described as being 'like a bird on its perch'. He is small, fragile, with a voice like a girl. He has lived in an army home for 60 years: alone, isolated, with other men all 'staring ahead of them'.

Tellingly, Elizabeth holds his hand, her first tangible connection with her past. Although Brennan's life seems empty it is an existence that chimes with her search: for him 'time became the present', and it is this attempt to recapture the past that reminds us of her quest. Brennan tells her of how Stephen held Douglas as he died, and it is this that is important because it reminds us of other episodes in the book (see p. 240) when the most important gesture we can make is to simply touch another person: it is this basic connection that sustains us. In listening to Brennan (and making physical contact with him) Elizabeth has 'somehow kept the chain of experience intact'.

Elizabeth is the catalyst for change in the book: it is she who explores the past, lives in the present and, becoming pregnant, looks to the future. Time — a major **theme** in the novel — is encapsulated in her. And in her lives hope: she concludes the novel, pushing out new life, and in a passage that echoes Stephen being torn from mother earth, Elizabeth creates a new life, but also a link with the past: this is the child that her grandfather promised Jack he would have for him, and Elizabeth names him after Jack's boy, John. It is Elizabeth's mother who provides the coda to the novel when she says of her life with Stephen and Jeanne: 'when there is real love between people, as there was between all of us, then the details don't matter' (p. 494).

There are many similarities and differences between Elizabeth and Isabelle, but it is clear that Faulks wants us to consider the contextual — or social and cultural — differences that allow for such contrasts. It would be easy to conclude that Isabelle is trapped because of the period and place she lived in and that, equally, Elizabeth is free for the same reason. But is it as simple as that? Isabelle seems braver than Elizabeth: it is she who follows her passions in first leaving Azaire for Stephen and then living with Max. Some might claim that such actions are reckless, but one thing that Isabelle does do is to accept the repercussions of her actions. Elizabeth's life, for all its independence, is perhaps even more compromised than Isabelle's: given the

comparative freedom she enjoys she seems unusually restricted and passive in her relationship with Robert. He seems to dictate the nature of their relationship; indeed, both female characters seem very passive in their relationships with male characters. Elizabeth also seems guided far more by her emotions than Isabelle: her desire to have a child is fundamental to her sense of self, and Faulks could be arguing that we are ruled by such basic urges and desires far more than by moral or intellectual concerns.

Themes

War and peace

Conflict is present at the very start of the novel. The first word that alerts us to this suggested violence is the mention of the River Somme, a place name that evokes the scene of perhaps the most infamous battle in British military history, and certainly the most tragic. It is a name that seems to explode on the page, filled as it is with endless associations of grief. We cannot view it with anything other than a sense of dread, regret and foreboding. The fact that this part of the novel is set in 1910 in France means that we cannot help but look ahead to what is about to happen. The weight of the war seems to explain the extreme action we are about to witness: the beating of Isabelle by Azaire, the intense passion between Isabelle and Stephen, the unrest in the town. Everything is pointing to the violence of what is to come, and life seems compressed into a period of shortened time; experience has to be crammed into as little time as possible because there is not much time left. As Geoff Dyer writes: 'the future presses on the lovers like the dead weight of geological strata. The Great War took place in the past — even when it lay in the future' (p. 84). In an atmosphere filled with portents, seemingly innocent incidents can become ominous: Bérard's songs at the end of the dinner party are sentimental ('One day the young men came back from the war/The corn was high and our sweethearts were waiting…'), even Isabelle's lust for Stephen is described in **imagery** close to that associated with conflict (she wanted him to 'demean, destroy, her fabricated self'), but because of the context they are filled with anticipatory irony. First impressions seem to count here: Azaire and Bérard are seen as false and untrustworthy. Both are bullies who abuse their power, and both are fated to die at the hands of the German Army. Indeed, Bérard is shown to be, in Stephen's words, 'a preposterous little man, full of his own importance' who lends his house to the German commandant when the town is invaded.

The scenes set in the trenches are considered by most readers to be the most powerful in the novel, and it is easy to see why. None of the soldiers are portrayed as conventionally 'heroic': they are, instead, recognisably human — vulnerable, stoical and scared. The shells that rain down night after night terrify them because they threaten to 'obliterate all physical evidence that a man had existed', and it is this loss of remembrance, this fear of being forgotten, that Faulks concentrates on in many of these passages. The shells 'unman' them, and when they do feel genuine fear they realise 'how unnatural…the existence they were leading; they did not wish to be reminded of normality' (p. 148); such emotions deepen the sense of alienation they feel and must be banished if they are to carry on. In these conditions some cannot, or will not, carry on, and Stephen and Weir are fascinating because although they are NCOs the reader is never really sure that they will not crack — or be destroyed — by a shell or stray bullet (as Weir is).

At the centre of the book is the Battle of the Somme, and it says much for Faulks's skill as a writer that he is able to describe this so effectively. The day is marked out by its unreality, by extremes: Colonel Barclay, like someone from an earlier age, carries a sword into a battle that also sees machine-made killing done on a monumental scale: the mine that Jack had been laying leaves the earth 'eviscerated…It was too big…the scale appalled him'. The conflict opens up a 'fresh world at the instant of its creation', he is reduced to walking into fire 'like an old woman' hunched against the inevitable tearing of flesh, his men resemble 'primitive dolls', one soldier — Hunt — is killed, 'his head opening up bright red', language that is deliberately distant, defamiliarised. Stephen himself begins to think of himself as 'floating above his body…it was as though he had become detached, in a dream, from the metal air through which his flesh was walking'. The 'broken ground' supports a shattered world and a dislocated perception: what is real and unreal seem to blur into each other, as do life and death, and so it is not odd to read of a man walking with part of his face missing, also in the 'same dreamlike state'.

Faulks's rendition of the battle as something unreal and, to some extent, unknowable, works extremely well: nobody who reads about the day, either in fiction or through primary historical sources, can appreciate how truly nightmarish it was. Faulks does not attempt to describe it in great detail; instead, he picks out surreal moments, episodes that highlight its absurd horror, and in doing so makes its depiction oddly, and frighteningly, believable.

Life, in this novel, seems to be a matter of chance: we only have to look at Weir's death to see how random acts of brutality can end life in a second. God is not a presence in this novel, in the sense that religion does not offer any sort of organised, systematic interpretation of existence. For some characters — such as Jack — there is an erosion of one's faith, and it would be a fair interpretation to say that survival, for some, is dependent on nothing more than luck. And yet it is not as simple as that. Obviously, Stephen is a central character in a work of fiction and as such his 'survival' is assured because it serves the purpose of the **plot**. One should always remember that a novel is a work of art, and the characters in it are constructs: candidates who write about Stephen or Isabelle as if they were real people, subject to the same vagaries as us, will be unable to write a good critical essay.

Having said that, Faulks is clearly not entirely convinced that life is decided purely through luck: he emphasises the link between the past, present and future (with Stephen, Elizabeth and John forming a clear and strong chain of destiny). We also feel, when we read certain passages, that characters have decided upon their fates and that this decisiveness has a greater influence on their fate than anything else (consider, for instance, Isabelle's decision to leave Azaire and then Stephen). Pattern — or order — does not impose meaning in this novel: indeed, the routine that the soldiers lead is shown to be deadening. But we are made aware by characters such as Stephen, Elizabeth and even Levi that life is filled with endless possibilities, but meaning is often only conferred retrospectively by those who survive to interpret it. We can take control of our lives: we can choose life (as Stephen does) or we can choose death (as Jack does), but such choices are often decided by personality, upbringing and experience.

Some readers feel that the passages set in 1978 are weak: they lack the impact of the sections set in war-torn France and they are filled with characters who are comparatively flat and uninteresting: Elizabeth's search for her past only partially convinces us because as a character she seems so passionless and aimless. Faulks obviously intends us to see how the past is inherently linked to the present and that we can only make sense of the one if we understand the other. The links are everywhere: we live in an environment that is physically, intellectually and morally shaped by the past and yet we often choose to ignore it, or at least overlook it, as Elizabeth has done until she finds Stephen's notebooks. It could be argued that the passages set in France during the war are intensified by those set in a Europe of peace, and that the double focus strengthens, through a series of contrasts, the novel. The lack of a chronological order reminds us that the past has not gone, but is still with us, shaping the future as it is discovered — and recovered — by the living.

Death is everywhere in the novel: it is the main canvas, around which are the frames of peacetime France and England. Faulks writes about death convincingly: it becomes mundane for some of the characters and its scale, at times, overwhelms, but those who die in war, Faulks seem to say, should be remembered, and we should still see that so many lives lost was an outrage — an outrage that Horrocks responds to (and which is apparently based on a true event) when he watches the British die in the Somme. But Faulks also threads imagery of death throughout the book. Look at the following passage:

> Jack had at first viewed the lice on his body as simple parasites whose presump-
> tions had made him indignant. The way they dug their ugly fawn-coloured
> bodies into the private pores of his skin had revolted him. He took great
> pleasure in holding a lighted candle and working it slowly up the seams of his
> clothes where the insects lurked and bred. Usually their fiery deaths were silent,
> though occasionally he would hear a satisfying crackle…If there was no candle
> available, a fiercely applied thumbnail was effective up to a point. There was a

sense of relief when some of the creatures were gone, though it was like the crushing of a blood-gorged mosquito: Jack always felt they had no right to be there in the first place. The evident advantage in cutting back the numbers was the temporary relief it gave from the sour, stale smell the creatures left, though even this relief was qualified, since the odour was usually compounded or over-whelmed by stronger and more persistent bodily smells.

There is a direct analogy being made here between the parasites and the lives of the soldiers, and in doing this Faulks is being deliberately provocative. 'Parasite' is an emotive term that has strong **connotations** of worthlessness: is this what Faulks means? Or does he mean that the lives of the soldiers are as disposable as these creatures? The creatures are, through being described as presumptuous, anthro-pomorphised to some extent, but their lives are brief and futile and they end violently. Tellingly, like the men they live on, their fates are 'fiery' or violent, and although killing them affords temporary relief, it is only temporary: more come, taking their place, and the process begins again, thus adding to the sense of futility. Faulks writes that Jack felt that 'they had no right to be there in the first place' and this is obviously a reference to the soldiers on both sides.

Social class

Class was an explosive ingredient in the British Army in both world wars: officers, who came from predominantly middle- to upper-class families, were placed, for the first time, in close proximity — and for prolonged periods of time — with the working-class soldiers below them. Tensions were inevitable, and they can be found in Faulks's narrative. The officers are all of the same class, although it could be argued that because of his unusual background, Stephen is to some extent 'classless'. Having said that, he is obviously the social superior to characters such as Jack, Shaw, Tyson and others.

Class is often a divisive factor in the novel: in France, for instance, the industrial dispute in Azaire's factory is about money and the workforce is recognisably of a lower class than Isabelle's family. Class is a factor in the animosity between the two sides and this is manifested in the secrecy Isabelle has to resort to in helping the striking dyers. Class divides societies, but in times of war it can often be overcome as a greater need takes hold, that of survival, something that Isabelle recognises (p. 110):

> She thought of all the mothers who lived in the villages that lined the narrow road leading from the town. Out there were millions of young men, strong, smiling, as her boy would be, working on the land. They never knew each other, never met, never considered any kinship or allegiance they might have to each other or to the country they lived in, because such things existed only in time of war.

Class is to be found in the trenches, and we see it as soon as Stephen encounters Jack Firebrace. The army is organised along class divisions: because of his background and

education it was inevitable that Stephen would enlist as an officer, just as it was accepted that Captain Gray would be able to 'acquire a batman [a military servant] called Watkins who had once trained as a chef in the kitchens of the Connaught Hotel in London' (p. 162).

Faulks appears to be happier writing about characters who are members of the middle class: Stephen and the other officers are rounded characters with, we feel, inner lives. Readers often react negatively to the representation of characters such as Jack and the other tunnellers: it could be said that they often do not rise above the level of **caricature**. One critic, Alice Ferrebe, has remarked that 'Jack's family…are fit to inspire little beyond a Dickensian pathos; a rather raddled older woman and a sickly child who is later to die of bronchitis' (*Re-visiting or Revisionist? A Comparative Reading of Gender Relationships in Selected First World War Novels*). This seems harsh though, because the weaknesses in some of the characterisation are not attributable to class alone; conversely, the strengths cannot simply be explained by the fact that Faulks understands their social milieu. Class is a strong theme in the novel, as it should be given how important it was in the First World War.

Faulks seems to be saying that we should not be defined by our class alone. One example is that of Jack and Stephen, who come from the working and middle classes respectively, and who end the book with a profound understanding of each other. Their lives, although very different, are also similar: they understand, at the end of their experience underground, the importance of love in life, and such concerns transcend differences in class.

A second example is when Isabelle is seen to support Lebrun's factory workers when they are on strike (in Part One). This shows not only her compassion, but also the gulf that exists between the classes. The simple urge to help others is fraught with difficulty: she is the boss's wife, she is a woman working alone and in the company of men, and she is part of the middle class. And yet the simple desire to help others is stronger than all these divisions.

Another example is that of Europe in 1978. This is a society that is markedly less restricted by class than the Europe of 60 years earlier. Elizabeth is able to talk to others in a recognisably equitable way. Class has become less important in this society, as have the expectations placed on women.

Human emotions are not restrained by class and sexual attraction: hatred, jealousy and love can overwhelm any barriers placed on individuals by class.

Sex and relationships

Sex scenes are notoriously difficult to write: indeed, many writers prefer to avoid them altogether, preferring instead the literary equivalent of the cinematic 'fade out'. The scenes in the red room are central to the development of the novel's characters and themes: for us to see Isabelle and Stephen as characters capable of a great passion we have to understand the extent to which they can discard their public personas; we must be swept along, to some extent, by the strength of their feelings. This is a novel of extremes: we see the limits of life, and it would be oddly jarring if a discreet veil was pulled over the moments of great intimacy. They also add to the plot: Lisette overhears them and tries to blackmail Stephen into beginning an affair with her; we are also expected to contrast their mutual and passionate love with the sadistic pleasure Azaire takes from beating Isabelle (and so ingrained is that impulse that Faulks writes that after discovering their affair, and in the process of throwing both of them out of his house, 'in the midst of his [Azaire's] anger and his humiliation, he noted the return of a low urge he had not felt for months'). Stephen and Isabelle are seen as liberated from oppression through love and sex. Whether or not this works depends to some extent on the expectations of the reader.

Stephen and Isabelle are the two characters with whom we most closely associate sexual intimacy, but they are not the only ones. Faulks asks us to consider how sex, like other powerful urges, can shape our perception of ourselves and each other. For example, when Lisette tries to seduce Stephen we are made aware just how powerful lust is: it threatens to destabilise everything, and it is ironic that it is Stephen, of all the characters, who understands the need to control it. He knows that it can set in motion a train of events that could be ruinous (on p. 88 Faulks writes: 'He pulled it [his hand] away at once because his inclination was to leave it there and he knew if he did so it would be the start of something more awful and more hopeless than he had already begun').

The trenches themselves would appear to be, at first glance, a sexless habitat, but there is physical intimacy between the men (between Firebrace and Shaw for example) and a perfunctory, functional need for the men to release their sexual frustration through resorting to using prostitutes. Sex exists in the trenches, as does love, but they are seldom linked: the war forces all the characters to be aware of how short time is, and to guard against forming any lasting relationships. It would be possible to see Weir's social unease as being, somehow, linked to his virginity. His fear of losing that virginity — to a prostitute — could be explained in many different ways: he could be homosexual, or he could be reluctant to give away, so cheaply, an essential part of his own identity.

What does Faulks want us to feel about sex? Probably nothing more than that it is a vital part of our identities, and that it is almost impossible to control if that sexual attraction for another person is reciprocated: all barriers collapse, but in doing so the social checks and balances, which are in place for good reason, are removed as well, and the damage done then can be extensive. There is nihilism to sex: it destroys and creates, and this is acknowledged by Stephen as he begins to fall in love with Isabelle: 'the sensation of desire seemed indistinguishable from an impulse towards death' (p. 45). We should also not forget Elizabeth: she appears to be the character who is most at ease with herself, both emotionally and sexually. Even so, she seems uncertain about how to form — or sustain — relationships.

Whether you consider that Elizabeth's attitude to sex is healthier than Isabelle's depends upon your moral position regarding sexual relationships. It is certainly more modern, but is it any less damaging? Neither Isabelle nor Elizabeth are involved in entirely happy relationships, and both women are mistresses. You do not have to be a feminist critic to see such a position as being essentially compromised, framed, as it were, by male demands and expectations. To put it simply, although the female characters in the novel exert some power, they are always secondary to the male characters, but whether this is a reflection of society, rather than an outmoded view of human relationships, is difficult to say. Elizabeth is free to have casual sex with a young man she meets on a walking holiday, just as she is free to have a child by another woman's husband, but the parallels between her position and Isabelle's are so clearly drawn as to suggest that this coupling of the characters' fates was Faulks's primary objective, and that any social **criticism** such a link introduces is not intended to be penetrating.

Innocence and experience

The conflict between innocence and experience is fundamental to understanding the novel. Childhood innocence gives way to adult experience in many works of literature, yet this novel extends it so that the divisions found in the domestic realm are also found, on a grander scale, in the trenches. Arguably, the novel is a study of the move from innocence to experience, both for the central characters and for the forces that fought each other over four years.

The characters who most obviously become more experienced — and disillusioned — are Stephen and Jack. Through a series of losses they realise just how fragile, and to some extent empty, life can be. Jack dies convinced that what is valuable has gone, whereas Stephen stays alive perhaps because his losses have not been so great. None of the characters who experience the war remain untouched by it. Indeed, even the minor characters leave us in no doubt that what they see on the battlefield shakes them to their core. A telling exchange takes place between Stephen and Gray after Stephen is injured (p. 341):

> 'I saw your face that July morning we attacked at Beaumont. I took my orders from you at the head of the communications trench.'
>
> 'And?'
>
> 'I looked in your eyes and there was perfect blankness.'
>
> Gray, for the first time since Stephen had known him, seemed wrong-footed. He coughed, and looked down. When he could meet Stephen's eye again, he said, 'Those are intimate moments.'
>
> Stephen nodded. 'I know. I was there. I saw the great void in your soul, and you saw mine.'

Such moments can best be termed epiphanies: sudden realisations that crystallise an experience, and the novel has many. We witness all the characters' moments of great insight as they move from 'innocence' to greater experience, and these are not described in a manner that suggests that Faulks sees such a journey as being anything other than painful and inevitable. For example, when Isabelle and Stephen admit to having an affair we are made aware of the damage done to those who are only witnesses. On p. 100 Faulks writes that 'they [Lisette and Grégoire] watched the wretched emotions of adulthood' unfold before their eyes, another step away from innocence, towards a greater, but less beautiful, view of life.

Isabelle, perhaps more than most, learns about herself through what she does — and what is done to her — but it would be wrong to think of her as 'innocent' to begin with. Her life, like Stephen's, has not been easy, and she has had to endure a great deal in her marriage to Azaire. She, more than any other character, seems to personify the Europe of the time: she is essentially passive at first, and finds herself torn between an Englishman and a German. Her destiny is only settled when she decides to follow her own wishes and fulfil her own destiny.

It could also be argued that Europe moves from innocence to experience: the opening section is bucolic and, because of the date and the place names, we are made very aware that this state is doomed. The suddenness of the shift is total: Europe is plunged into a cataclysmic war that will change the world forever. In contrast, the characters' experiences seem relatively unimportant, but they are seen as being intrinsically linked to — as well as separate from — the context they function within. They are seen to live and develop in wartime just as, superficially, they might do in peacetime: they fall in and out of love, have sex, make friends and enemies, eat, drink, sleep, gain promotion, dream, write letters, even go shopping, but all of it is conducted against a backdrop of war. This is important because Faulks has to show us that although the war was indeed an awful — and drawn-out — episode in man's history, life had to continue as well.

In *Birdsong* change is often seen in negative terms: Europe moves from a state of relative peace to one of chaos and death. How could this be viewed as anything other than in bleak, even nihilistic, terms? Yet there is optimism at the end of the war, which is criticised by some as being unrealistic. Yes, Europe changes, and the continent that is described in 1978 is preferable to the one that we see in 1918. There seems to be more freedom, more affluence and more freedom of movement. The question is whether this change has been bought at too high a price: were those deaths, which Elizabeth begins to be made aware of when she visits the Albert Memorial, worth it? Only if we remember how such change comes about. Elizabeth's personal odyssey is necessary because it allows her to reconnect with the past: change is only truly negative if we do not understand or remember what we have lost and gained in the process.

Identity and belonging

Place is fundamental to understanding this novel. The place names in prewar France reek of the conflict that is about to be forever associated with them. Place cannot be disassociated from our understanding of what is about to occur: doom seems to be waiting in the wings, prefiguring the outcome of the action. It seems unlikely that anything good will spring from a place as closely associated with death as the Somme, and even when Stephen and Isabelle elope, the names they pass are beaten out like a death march: 'a second train took them from Albert out along the small country line beside the Ancre, past the villages of Mesnil and Hamel to the station at Beaucourt' (p. 83). Faulks is unusual for an English writer in that he locates much of his fiction in France, rather than his homeland. One senses that this is a writer who is constantly searching for what it means to belong, for what constitutes individual identity. What do we mean by home? How does our relationship with our surroundings shape our sense of self? Faulks admits (in Noakes, J. and Reynolds, M. (eds) (2002) *Sebastian Faulks: The Essential Guide*, Vintage Living Texts, p. 16.) that 'places are very much part of the initial throb of the idea for me' when he plans a book. For Faulks place suggests 'incidents which might happen'. For him, place comes before character and, to a great extent, the truth of a novel begins with its location: it has to be, in many ways, real and convincing, and once that is established the characters are added. But these characters constantly relate to their surroundings, particularly in moments of extreme emotion: for instance, when Stephen bursts through the cut wire in the Somme, he is overwhelmed not just with a joy of being alive, but also for being in this 'piece of field beneath a French heaven' (p. 227).

Faulks admits that the theme of a lost home recurs throughout the novel: Stephen is homeless, and Isabelle becomes homeless. Indeed, none of the major characters really belong in any one place, and this sense of rootlessness explains, to some extent, their feeling of disorientation, which is exacerbated by the war. Stephen and Isabelle 'find themselves' in the red room, and this becomes, in many ways, an inner sanctum, a place of great intimacy at the core of their inner lives. Places function symbolically as well. It is no coincidence that Azaire himself did not really consider the red room, that place of passion (p. 100):

> He had not thought of the red room. He [Azaire] had forgotten the narrow corridor with its plain wooden boards that doubled back from the garden side of the house towards the back stairs. Since he had first bought the house he had had no cause to visit it, had never in fact seen its finished shape, such as it was, after it had been cleared of the previous owners' unwanted belongings and modestly redecorated by Isabelle. It was a place he had not refound, but which had stayed, as Stephen feared it might for him, beyond the reach of memory.

The room is linked to lust, to the sexual urge that Azaire and Isabelle have never shared, and possibly also to that first home as well: the womb, again, a barren place for Isabelle and Azaire. It is all the more symbolic that it is destroyed by a bomb as the city is fought over by the Allied and German forces: it symbolises the destruction of that sense of home that Stephen and Isabelle shared momentarily. Other characters who seem to be distant from their surroundings include Jack Firebrace and Michael Weir, both of whom die in a country that, surprisingly, they seem to understand more than the England they have left behind. Even Elizabeth seems unfamiliar with her context: the Europe that she explores is largely unknown to her, and it is only by reading her grandfather's journals that she begins to see how she has been shaped by her past; however, whether she belongs or not is open to dispute and, perhaps tellingly, she removes herself to a hired cottage — an emotional 'no man's land' — to have her first child. Stephen settles in Norfolk for no real reason other than it appealed to him when he travelled through it on leave. Nobody seems to truly belong in their homes in this novel, and that search for 'home', whatever or whoever that may turn out to be, points to an ongoing search for contentment, something that remains an elusive quality, not just in *Birdsong*, but in other works by Faulks.

The extent to which you see Isabelle's love for Max as a betrayal of her country depends on how you view an individual's duty to their homeland. It is not uncommon for men and women from different 'sides' of a conflict to fall in love: after all, individuals, rather than countries, love or hate each other. But Isabelle's love for Max obviously has symbolic significance that transcends the purely personal, and in many ways it parallels Stephen's embracing of Levi at the end of the novel: both acts are moments of reconciliation and, to some extent, forgiveness. Some readers might feel that both 'relationships' are symptomatic of a 'soft' or idealistic core at the heart of the novel; they might argue that the message that Faulks seems to be conveying is that we are, through a shared humanity, capable of overcoming inherited prejudices, and that such a belief, although admirable, is unrealistic, especially during a war. But where hope does exist in the novel it exists here, not between nations, but between individual characters. However, even this hope feels doomed: Isabelle and Max do not 'live happily ever after', and Stephen's embracing of Levi seems at best transient and at worst futile in its significance when one considers how Jewish people will be treated in Europe within 20 years of the end of the war. The clouds of the next conflict were gathering as the peace was spreading across a shattered Europe. The love between individuals could not stop this.

Fate and free will

> Sometimes Stephen felt his body was no more than a channel for exterior
> powers; it had no proper sense of fatigue or proportion. (p. 90)

Like many themes that one explores in the study of literature, how we perceive fate and free will depends largely on whether we believe in it or not. That said, it is also true that a character in a novel is 'fated' to lead a life set for him by the author. If

we leave this aside as being too obvious (and unhelpful) for literary analysis, we have to look at the ontological concerns of the writer: to what extent are characters' fates shaped by their actions and thoughts? To some extent Stephen manipulates his own fate and this distinguishes him from other characters: he seems to take an active control of his life, even saying to Weir at one point: 'I fix the cards. I cheat.' Weir, in contrast, believes that there is a pattern to life, and that Stephen reveals or predicts it. To some extent Stephen seems to be the instigator of much of the action: he refuses to be passive, preferring instead to try to seize control of his life, and he has done this from the beginning of the novel. The series of tunnels, both at the beginning of the novel (in Azaire's house) and at the end (in the trenches), act as a linking symbol to suggest paths not taken. We are constantly being made to think about both the choices (see, for example, p. 453).

Whether or not there is a predetermined set of paths that we have no control over is fundamental to a soldier's view of his fate. The 'bullet with my name on it' is not just a flippant phrase: it is something believed in by many because it imposes order on chaos. Whether or not Stephen believes in this is uncertain: '"Sometimes," said Stephen… "I do believe in a greater pattern. In different levels of experience; a belief in the possibility of an explanation"', but his analysis does not go much further than this. What is seen as dangerous by the military authorities is Stephen's dabbling with 'hocus pocus' because, although it might comfort some (most obviously Weir), it is, at its heart, profoundly destabilising because it challenges the basis of military planning. Gray says to him at one point that 'Officers are not superstitious, Wraysford. Our lives depend on strategy and tactics, not matchsticks or card games' (p. 192). The truth is that their lives depend as much on luck — or fate — as anything else. But because soldiers follow orders they do subscribe to a greater power organising life: they have to believe that the plans put in place have some sense because if they think otherwise — if they feel that there is no plan, but only chance — then their whole belief system collapses, much as it did for Weir and Jack. To some extent they are reduced to the condition of children, and Gray recognises this when he says to Stephen: 'I think children need to believe in powers outside themselves.' If that power is absent — be it the parent, the CO, or God — then we are alone. Does this matter? To the characters in this novel it does, because, as Stephen asks: 'Who knows? Our own choices might not be as good as those who are made for us.'

In *Birdsong* character, to some extent, is fate, and this is nowhere more clearly seen than when we assess the character of Elizabeth. Her link with her past exposes just how much of our lives is linked to our forefathers: we see her life, and the life she gives birth to at the end, as fated to be because she is Stephen's granddaughter. The same could be said of us all: none of us would be alive today if certain decisions had not been taken in the past that brought together the particular set of circumstances that resulted in our being born. It is hard not to believe in fate when we look at our own genealogy. And yet Faulks — through Weir, Jack, Byrne, and others — warns us away from such conclusions. That we are alive today is as much chance as anything else. We may place a pattern on it, but we have to be aware of just how much of that pattern is derived from our own desire to draw meaning from chaos.

It could be argued that for a soldier to be able to fight for his country he must feel as if he belongs to that country first. Yet the characters in *Birdsong* seem, at different stages of the novel, disillusioned with England. The most obvious example is Stephen: he has no particular affinity with England, but decides to fight for his homeland, rather than France, because he cannot imagine fighting alongside the French. He is motivated by a hatred of Germans rather than a love of the English. Neither he nor Weir ever claim to be fighting to defend England; indeed, Weir would be happy if 'a great bombardment would smash down along Piccadilly into Whitehall and kill the whole lot of them', such is his disgust with civilian English life. What Faulks shows us is that war not is an idealistic crusade: causes are for politicians and generals, not the men on the front line. A soldier has no choice other than to fight for his country: if he chose not to fight at this time he would be shot. The choices were as stark as that, and because of this dilemma it is not surprising that the characters exist in a sort of existential hell: they are very aware of the emptiness of their lives and see it, in many ways, as futile, but there is no alternative except death. It is not surprising that the experience of the trenches — when fighting men were kept against their will for long periods of passivity alternating with extreme danger — led to a crisis in society once peace had been declared. There was, as Philip Larkin has written, never such innocence again, and nor was there the blind allegiance to the flag that characterised the initial rush to join up to fight.

Remembrance

Remembrance is as much a part of the fabric of the Great War as the images of the doughty Tommy, the poppies, the trenches, the last post. We remember, and when we remember we have Binyon's lines in our heads:

> They shall grow not old, as we that are left grow old:
>
> Age shall not weary them, nor the years condemn.
>
> At the going down of the sun and in the morning
>
> We will remember them.
>
> R. L. Binyon, 'For the Fallen'

But how do we remember those we did not know? What emotions go through us when we hear Binyon's poem? What do we think about when we stand in silence for a minute? Why are many of us moved when we hear the Last Post? Only a very small number of people alive today have any direct connection with the First World War, although we may have family members who died or were injured in the conflict.

Birdsong asks us to think about how inseparable memory is from identity. Just as a country that does not seek to remember its dead loses a vital part of its own identity, so too an individual who cannot recall his or her past is denied an essential part of his or her own makeup. From almost the start of the novel Jack's memory is beginning to fade: he is becoming removed from his past, and this indicates a deep sense of loss that culminates in his death (which can, to some extent, be accounted for by his acceptance that what he once remembered had gone). The emotions that the men experience are so intense that they seem to wipe out more fragile mental images. On pp. 127–28 Faulks writes:

> In the murk of the rainy evening, with only Tyson's piece of candle for light, it was difficult to see. He closed his eyes and pictured his son's knees beneath the ragged grey shorts, the big teeth he revealed when he smiled, the untidy hair through which he would sometimes run a fatherly hand…There was always too much to think of to allow his mind to dwell on the inessentials.

And yet it is the inessentials that keep us going: the link with the past is a valuable thread of life. We know that Jack is in effect dying from within when Faulks writes that 'he could not remember John's face well enough to draw it' (p. 372). That disconnection is symbolic of a deeper malaise.

Elizabeth works in the opposite direction: her motivation is, to a great extent, to recapture the past (she says on p. 250 that she feels as if 'there's a danger of losing touch with the past') and that is why she acts. She seeks to remember that which she has never known, and her discovery of Stephen's notebooks allows her to do this. We watch her discover her past, and in doing so she unearths a part of herself that reshapes her view of the present and the future. Faulks seems to be saying that although remembrance is difficult, we have to strive to understand what it means: these people did suffer and die, and they were just like us, and if we look closely enough — at the memorials, even at the everyday signs of the past — we will discover more about ourselves.

Masculinity and femininity

There is no more 'masculine' activity than war, and yet Faulks shows us in this novel how the conflict not only affects women and children, but also profoundly challenges what it means to be a man in the twentieth century.

Isabelle is the most obvious female victim of the war: her scarred face is a living testimony to the battle she has been caught up in, and she also loses her husband. Even when she falls in love the relationship is, due to the war, defined as unacceptable because her lover is German. To some extent she is representative of widows across the continent. Even those we do not see, such as Jack's wife, Margaret, are diminished by the war. The lowly prostitutes who service the soldiers at the front are also victims of the war. And yet these women desperately try to retain what scraps of dignity they have. It is perhaps Isabelle's sister, Jeanne, who is strengthened by the war: it is she who offers support to her sister, to Stephen, and it is she who finds love. Elizabeth seems more liberated than these women, and it is certainly true that she is independent and free from overt male oppression. Yet she is also, to some extent, exploited as a mistress by Robert and controlled by her urge for children and marriage. The expectations placed on women at the end of the twentieth century, although less severe, would nonetheless be recognisable to anyone who lived in 1918.

The male characters are often reduced to caricatures of what it means to be a man: they fight, they drink, they have sex with prostitutes and yet, ironically, they are powerless. For much of the war they sit underground, lonely and frustrated, seemingly abandoned by the country they are fighting to defend. The long periods of passivity, alternating with extreme violence, render them almost incapable of forming normal relationships, either with each other or with women. Indeed, Stephen says to Weir on p. 151 that women 'belong to a different existence'. And yet that desire for men and women to be with each other is a primitive urge which is impossible to deny. We see it when Stephen and Weir visit the mother and daughter prostitutes: Stephen looks at the younger woman and thinks that there is 'air and life in her limbs. The flesh was young and unwounded. He wanted to drown himself in her, to bury deep into the cells of her skin and to forget himself there. She was peace and gentleness; she was the possibility of love and future generations'. Sex allows both characters very different experiences, but once it is over the reality of the war reasserts itself: for Stephen the girl's upper body reminds him 'of the shell casing that stuck from Reeves's abdomen…tenderness was replaced at first by a shuddering revulsion'.

The war makes all the characters victims in one way or another, and Faulks is asking us to look beyond the obvious — and terrible — casualties of the Somme. The men who went to war were there because it was seen then — and to some extent still is — as a man's role to fight, and to that extent they are victims. But other factors complicate matters: class, for instance, plays a role in deciding what fate they might expect at the Front. The female characters are also victims, and the fact that they are women narrows their opportunities: they are vulnerable; they are liable, like Isabelle, to becoming pregnant and having their lives dictated by men. Yet, as Stephen says, this propensity to give life rather than take it away marks them out as the symbols of true hope in the novel.

There are two births in this novel: Isabelle gives birth to Françoise (Elizabeth's mother) and Elizabeth gives birth to John (Stephen's great-grandson). The hope that they represent is unambiguous: such births embrace the future and, in Elizabeth's decision to name her son after Jack's son, they also connect the past with the present. Stephen is reborn at least twice in the novel (there are other, less clear transformations, such as his transformation from a young and disillusioned man into a self-confident officer, or his reawakening into the spoken world after two years

of silence). He is reborn after a heavy bombardment and is rescued by Jack, who finds him naked 'except for one boot and a disc around his neck'. The second time he is reborn occurs at the end of the novel when he is plucked from the earth by Levi, with 'the sound of life calling to him on a distant road'. These seem to be moments of resurrection, episodes that give testament to the human desire to survive. The other most obvious 'rebirth' occurs right at the end of the novel, when Elizabeth gives birth to her son, John.

Religion

> I think God needs us more than we need him. It's all about absence, isn't
> it?…They say that someone is most intensely present just after they have left.

Sebastian Faulks, *Engleby*

In an interview Faulks has said that 'it's not quite right to say that God is felt only as an absence'. He argues that the rejection of God by some of the characters is 'reasonable', given what is experienced. It would be historically inaccurate to claim that faith did not provide essential sustenance to many who fought in the Great War, but it is not Faulks's intention to be fair to all positions, nor is it possible in a single novel.

There are several obvious moments when religion is foregrounded by Faulks in this novel. The most obvious 'religious' figure is Jack Firebrace (indeed the first time we meet him he is on a cross), and when Horrocks throws down his cross when he witnesses the slaughter of the Somme we are forced to think about the crisis of faith that occurred for many during the war. But there are other, perhaps more effective, episodes that bear analysis.

On pp. 71–72, when Stephen is contemplating his new life with Isabelle, he decides to visit the cathedral, although he himself has no faith. It is here that he has a premonition:

> He was standing at the back of the cold cathedral, looking towards the choir
> stalls and the window in the east…He sat down on a chair and held his face in
> his hands. He saw a picture in his mind of a terrible piling up of the dead. It
> came from his contemplation of the church, but it had its own clarity: the row
> on row, the deep rotting earth hollowed out to hold them, while the efforts of
> the living, with all their works and wars and great buildings, were no more than
> the beat of a wing against the weight of time.

> He knelt forward on the cushion on the floor and held his head motionless in
> his hands. He prayed instinctively, without knowing what he did. Save me from
> that death. Save Isabelle. Save all of us. Save me.

Religion here is seen as something instinctual, perhaps a desperate impulse that, given the appropriate circumstances, can be found in all of us, regardless of what we say about the extent of our faith: it is the hope that something has control over our lives. Ironically, part of this prayer is met: Stephen and Isabelle are saved from the mass burials of the Great War, although Isabelle dies later in the great influenza epidemic. The cathedral, although it does not offer much comfort, at least imposes some dignity through remembrance, a fragile permanence that holds out against the waves of eternity. The premonition foreshadows the conflict to come and, perhaps intentionally (given Stephen's later experiments with fortune telling), marks the central character out as one who is unusually sensitive and prescient.

Isabelle also experiences an epiphany in a religious setting. Shortly after visiting the doctor to check if she is having a miscarriage she too decides to visit a religious building and experiences a very different moment of realisation (pp. 113–14):

> On the way back to the house, Isabelle stopped at the church and sat in a pew at the back. She had no further desire to confess to the priest, but she wanted to admit, if only to herself, her feelings of guilt about the way she had abandoned herself to physical pleasure.

> …She looked at the altar where a wooden crucifix was lit by candles, the waxy flesh below the ribs pierced and bleeding from the Roman soldier's spear. She thought how prosaically physical this suffering had been: the punctured skin on forehead, feet, hands, the parting of flesh with nails and steel. When even the divine sacrifice had been expressed in such terms, it was sometimes hard to imagine in what manner precisely human life was supposed to exceed the limitations of pulse, skin and decomposition.

Again, it is a religious context, and religious imagery, that inspires this contemplation of the divine and the mortal. Like Stephen — and like Jack and Horrocks — it is at critical moments in one's life when we are forced to consider the reality, the meaning of religion in our lives, and sometimes it is comforting and at others is found to be wanting. Faulks is forcing us to understand how it is impossible to be neutral when faced with death. However, it is not quite as simple as this, because Faulks uses the imagery of conception — the parting of flesh, of pulse — to show us that life and death are intricately connected: this moment of contemplation is, after all, inspired by a pregnant woman's fear that she is about to lose her child. At this point — caught between life and death — it is appropriate for the character to contemplate the iconography that attempts to make sense of suffering. Faulks's view of religious faith seems to be bound up with suffering; indeed, on p. 27, he writes that Bérard's Aunt Elise seems to encapsulate a hardened faith forged from real experience: 'her blackened mouth and harsh voice…seemed to embody a minatory spiritual truth, that real faith is not to be found in the pale face of the anchorite but in the ravaged lives of those who have had to struggle to survive'. In other words, if there is such a thing as spiritual truth then it exists in those who have lived against the odds: Stephen will go on to achieve such a state later on, and in doing so comes to understand the value of life. However, that does not bring him — or Faulks — any nearer to God.

Images and symbols

Imagery is a general term used to cover the use of language in representing many things, including feelings, thoughts, states of mind, objects, actions, the senses and so on. An image is not simply limited to a mental 'picture': it can be non-visual, complex, employing different senses to convey its power. Images are often conveyed using figurative language.

A symbol is an object that represents something else (and it can represent many different things simultaneously). We use symbols all the time; indeed, some would argue that life is so complex that it can only be understood through a series of symbols: think of a dove symbolising peace, a swastika symbolising Nazism, a poppy symbolising remembrance.

Birdsong makes great use of imagery associated with war, as well as other areas of life, and when you read the novel carefully you should note Faulks's use of key recurrent images, which add to the novel's **tone**. He uses several key symbols as well. Here are some of the more important symbols:

Birds and birdsong

There are several striking images associated with birds in this novel. Most obviously, Stephen has had a phobia about birds ever since he forced himself to touch a dead crow when he was a child. The imagery of birds — which are traditionally associated with innocence, beauty, nature and freedom — is subverted by Faulks. We read of the newly dead Byrne 'like a flapping crow on the wire'. Birds also contrast with the horror of what is being experienced at the time, revealing how nature is indifferent to our fate. This has been remarked upon by Faulks:

> In the midst of this awful slaughter you suddenly found that there'd be a fox snuffling around, or you'd hear a lark singing, and it underlines nature's utter indifference to human beings and what they do.

The birds caught in this conflict are still free to rise above it, and in doing so they remind those who fight of how trapped in one element they are ('a lark was singing in the unharmed air above', p. 485). It is telling that when, at the end of the novel, Robert leaves the house, elated at seeing his new son, John, being born, he picks up some conkers — a link with his own past — and throws them into the sky, inadvertently disturbing a roosting crow, thus emphasising that symbolic link with Stephen. In using deliberately violent language suggestive of the war, Faulks writes that it 'erupted from the branches with an explosive bang of its wings'. Its 'ambiguous call', being both grating and fluent, is heard 'by those still living', suggesting that life remains precious, transient and fragile, and is surrounded by reminders and symbols of death. Ultimately, the birdsong is a song of hope, but it also reminds us of how trapped we are, both by ourselves and our circumstances. However, tellingly, the only time when there is a noticeable absence of birdsong is on the morning of the Battle of the Somme: 'there was for once no sound of birds' (p. 224).

Colour

Colour is a complex symbol in a lot of literature: a colour can convey any number of emotions and associations and can be endlessly subtle. Faulks uses the same colour in different ways, but some — most obviously red — are associated with passion and, in particular, Isabelle. The red creeper on p. 4 hints at the strong emotions that are concealed within the walls, and Faulks's use of this colour deepens our understanding of the characters and some of the main themes. He writes that 'Madame Azaire wore a cream skirt with a dark red patterned waistcoat over a white blouse with an open neck', and this strong use of contrasts makes her vivid and memorable. But it is the red room itself that is most redolent of sexual desire. Stephen views it as 'one of those he had once seen but could never refind; it would be like a place in a dream that remains out of reach; it would always be behind him' (p. 58). Red is the colour of passion but also, for the still repressed Isabelle, of shame. When she blushes (p. 69):

> Her stomach and breasts turned red beneath her dress as the blood beat the skin in protest at her immodesty. It rose up her neck and into her face and ears, as though publicly rebuking her for her most private actions. It cried out in the burning red of her skin; it begged for attention.

She grows out of this inhibited state and becomes a more fulfilled woman; she is described as 'resplendent...in her oxblood skirt and linen waistcoat' (p. 106).

Isabelle seems to emanate passion, but it is hidden (or coded), seen by an observer receptive to its every sign: Stephen notes on p. 84 that Isabelle 'was grafted to him, in flesh and in feeling. There was the high collar of her dress with the dull red stone at the throat'. Red is also the colour of blood, and Isabelle's view of herself is bound up with her menstrual cycle, which is seen, by her and Azaire, as a monthly failure. It is only when she meets Stephen and becomes pregnant that she is able to change her view of the colour and of herself (p. 109):

> It was hard to think of blood as the mark of new life, of hope...now in the withholding of it there was a sense of being healed. She had stopped haemorrhaging herself away; her power was turned inwards where it would silently create.

Such a complex colour takes her — and the reader — to areas of uncertain experience, or premonition; red acts as a connective between reality and imagined experience. It blurs life and death, for instance, when Stephen pours some 'reddish brown' water, 'contaminated by earth and blood' into a dying boy's 'beseeching mouth'. When Isabelle thinks of leaving Azaire (p. 101), she:

> ...dreamed of pale faces beneath rose-coloured lights; Lisette at the corner of the stairs, the bloodless features in the red glow, a lost girl, and others like her

caught in some repeated loop of time, its pattern enforced by the rhythmic
motion of the train; many white-skinned faces with dark eyes, staring in disbelief.

The colour reiterates the seriousness of the moment, and allows us to contemplate
the coming war, inadvertently caught up as it is with personal loss and betrayal.

Red, more than most colours, is forever linked with the war: it is worn every
year in this country to symbolise remembrance and, consciously or not, that red is
linked with the blood that soaked the fields in Europe.

Crosses

There are few symbols as potent as the cross. In *Birdsong* it is closely associated with
life and death, reminding characters of what they once believed in, or should aspire
to; it also symbolises what they have lost. On p. 113 Isabelle is sitting in a church
thinking of the oral sex she had performed on Stephen ('she could see Stephen's
blood-swollen flesh in front of her face'), and when she opens her eyes she sees in
front of her 'a wooden crucifix…lit by candles, the waxy flesh below the ribs pierced
and bleeding'. There is a direct correlation here between the body of man and the
body of Christ: the one is associated with mutual indulgence and sensuality, the
other with selflessness, pain and sacrifice. Faulks goes on to write about the 'prosaic'
parting of the flesh (p. 114) used to inflict pain, but again there is a direct link,
through this use of language, with penetrative sex. This is not to say that Faulks is
suggesting that a life dedicated to the spiritual is any more valuable than one that
lacks any faith; instead he is drawing our attention to the link between life and death,
suffering and guilt.

We meet Jack Firebrace on a wooden cross as he is pushed and pulled about
underground. But he is no Christ: his job is to ensure maximum damage, and when
he faces a court martial over falling asleep on duty his fear of death is real: he prays
that Shaw and Tyson, his friends, are taken, not him: 'let them die, but please God
let me live'. Jack loses his faith when he witnesses the Somme and when he loses
his son, and before he dies he begs Stephen to 'get me off this cross'. He moves
from a position of faith to one of spiritual emptiness. Jack is not the only character
who loses his faith in the Somme: most powerfully of all Horrocks, the padre,
'pulled the silver cross from his chest and hurled it from him. His old reflex still
persisting, he fell to his knees, but he did not pray…Jack knew what had died in
him' (p. 230). The cross, a symbol of faith, here symbolises the loss of faith in a
world that has to question the profound indifference the universe feels for the
suffering of mankind.

Crosses represent, for readers and film viewers, the countless deaths and sheer
waste of the First World War, with endless rows of them marking graves in war
cemeteries.

Tunnels

The novel is filled with passageways and tunnels: the Azaires' house on the Boulevard du Cange has many passageways and corridors filled with 'unseen footsteps'. On a very superficial level the house is built for deception and duplicity, but passageways and tunnels represent movement between states: from the surface to the hidden, from the open to the secret and concealed, from the conscious to the subconscious. All of the corridors and tunnels that we see in the novel act in the same way: they move characters from one state of being to another, and none of them emerge unchanged. Even Elizabeth is first encountered by the reader in a tunnel, thus connecting her with her past (at an unconscious level). Each tunnel also represents death and rebirth because each is, in effect, a ready-made grave waiting for its occupants: for Stephen to be dragged out at the end of the novel marks a new dawn, for him and Europe. But Faulks is not idealistic enough to try to convince us that such a fate allows us to forget the many — including Jack — who died in the tombs they dug with their own hands.

Language and structure

Style

For much of the novel Faulks's writing style is naturalistic and realistic. Like many writers, Faulks uses a number of narrative devices and switches from the third person omniscient narrator to the first person when he wants to add a greater degree of intimacy and authenticity. Faulks's influences include Emile Zola, whose novels, *Germinal* (1885), *La Terre* (1887), and *La Débâcle* (1892), show mankind's struggle against the overwhelming forces of the universe. Zola's subject matter and style has influenced Faulks's own work in that he shows, through language and theme, how experience is often incapable of deciphering — or making sense of — its context. In other words, naturalism attempts to convey the meaninglessness and randomness, as well as despair, of human life, which is not in control of its own destiny. The mixture of narrative perspectives appears at first to verify the authenticity of the experiences because they are represented through different voices, but each only confirms the central dilemma of existence.

Much of the important action in *Birdsong* is conveyed through notes, letters and journal entries (including Stephen's account of his life), through which we are forced to consider more closely the emotions and thoughts of the central characters. For the most part it is successful because it helps us to understand, at key points, their motives, emotions, actions and ideas. Such insights are also among the most moving in the whole novel: Isabelle's letter to Jeanne explaining why she left Azaire,

or Jack's final letter to Margaret that articulates his thoughts about their son, could only be written in the first person, and much of their power is derived from this narrative position. However, one unavoidable paradox of mixing narrative viewpoints is that it draws attention to the apparent artificiality of the third person narrator: Faulks's voice, although intense and often intimately involved, is more distant than these first person narratives. We are also left with the question of why Stephen's story, which is, apparently, written in the first person and translated by Bob, is written in the third person.

Characters' voices

Both Jack and Stephen are naturally taciturn, introspective characters. Nevertheless, both explore complex and important ideas: to themselves, with other characters, and to each other. Characters such as Elizabeth and Weir are more outspoken and emotionally expressive, but it is Jack and Stephen who give voice to the more profound emotions in the novel; inevitably, it is they who are thrown together at the book's climax to discuss the worth of love and life from two very different perspectives. Both are buried alive at the end of the novel and only Stephen survives. Jack's inarticulacy is accentuated by his injury: his legs are crushed and, unlike Stephen, he communicates in broken, incomplete sentences. When he does discuss complex emotions, such as fatherhood and loss, his **idiolect** seems to slip, and he switches from a blunt, matter-of-fact vernacular to something more lyrical (pp. 451–52):

> I loved that boy. Every hair of him, every pore of his skin. I would have killed a man who so much as laid a hand on him. My world was in his face…I treasured each word he gave me…he was from another world, he was a blessing too great for me.

This is undoubtedly moving, but it seems to lack a certain authenticity: the voice does not chime with what we have experienced so far because it seems too philosophical, even poetical; furthermore, Stephen's promise to Jack that he will have Jack's children for him is the sort of statement that serves a purpose for the plot (the pregnant Elizabeth thinks that 'it was hard not to feel that it had in some sense pre-existed her') but, again, this seems out of character and, given the context, both insensitive and nonsensical. Both characters seem to change into something unrecognisable when they are forced together underground, and although it is conceivable that this could be because they are placed in extreme conditions that result in an unusual degree of intimacy, another explanation could be that for both to be able to converse and arrive at commonly agreed truths, both have to lose their distinctive voices and, in turn, part of the identities that Faulks has sedulously built up over the course of the whole novel.

It appears that Faulks is more comfortable with middle-class characters than he is with working-class ones: the **diction** of the former is closer to his own background, and Jack can often appear to be slow-witted and ponderous because he lacks the casual lucidity of Stephen. Characterisation is often strained in this novel and nowhere more so than when Jack wrestles with his loss of faith. Most novelists are highly educated and, by the very nature of their craft, articulate, therefore it is unsurprising that they sometimes struggle to write convincingly about inarticulate characters. That said, it could be argued by some that writers can only write about experiences they have had themselves: by logical extension a white, middle-class male writer could not write about, say, a black working-class woman. The history of literature shows that this is neither desirable nor true. Yet Jack does fail to convince in many ways, and is certainly less 'rounded' than Stephen.

The characters' use of language is not distinct to them alone: for instance, Elizabeth is, in almost every sense, the same as the other female characters in the sections set in modern-day England. However, differences are found between the characters' thoughts, responses, ideas, and emotions, all of which are explored through the omniscient narrator. Their voices become more distinctly their own when they are able to write their thoughts down, but for much of the novel individual voices are sublimated to plot and theme.

Setting

One critic, Michael Gorra, writing in the *New York Times*, commented that the sections set in modern-day England were weak: '…it is as if Mr. Faulks had bled his own prose white, draining it of emotion in order to capture the endless enervating slog of war.' Gorra is not alone in claiming that the modern-day sections are less powerful than those set in the war, but to some extent this is inevitable given the intensity of the latter, and they are necessary to relieve the reader from the often extremely moving and demanding pages involving Stephen and Weir, Jack et al. The reader has to decide if the novel would have been unsustainable — as a narrative — if it had not had such interspersed sections. Perhaps more interestingly, the reader is asked to compare and contrast our comparatively comfortable lives with those of our forefathers and to ask if the sacrifices made by that generation were worth it, and if they are now remembered.

Many consider the scenes set in the trenches as the most powerful in the novel. Faulks heightens our expectation of what is to come by setting the episodes in France, specifically in 1916, a date that is closely associated with the Somme. The tension in these pages reaches an almost unbearable pitch: the language is perfectly judged, and the action moves at great speed. At the heart of what is happening lies a sense of unpredictability: we feel that none of the characters are safe (something confirmed when Weir is shot, suddenly, by a sniper). Minor characters such as Tipper (p. 147) are injured in a casual and brutal way, as are others such as Shaw and Tyson.

The letters that the men write home to their loved ones (pp. 220–23) only add to the rising sense of climax: they are, in their own very different ways, moving and

revealing. All seem to be infused with a sense of foreboding, a dread that we share with them. Stephen's is the most articulate letter, and it is he who establishes the tone of what is to come: 'Some crime against nature is about to be committed' (p. 222), and we see this clearly when the bombardment begins.

At its peak on p. 225, Faulks writes 'the air overhead was packed solid with noise that did not move. It was as though waves were piling up in the air but would not break. It was like no sound on earth. Jesus, said Stephen, Jesus, Jesus'. On this page the paragraphing seems to break down into shorter units; the sentences seem incomplete: 'Stephen ducked. Men shouting.' Faulks mixes the absurd (Colonel Barclay carrying a sword) with the tragic ('Two men were clipping vainly with their cutters among the corpses, their movement bringing the sharp disdainful fire of a sniper. They lay still', p. 227) and reveals — in brutal, unflinching detail that Owen himself felt was a writer's moral obligation — the 'pity of war' . The chaos conveyed is almost unbearable to read but, at the same time, it is strangely compelling: it is almost impossible to stop reading it, propelled as we are by a desire to find out what happens to the characters and a certain knowledge that, because this is a novel set in a specific historical context, the outcome is predetermined and, in this instance, inevitable and bleak.

Literary terms and concepts

The terms and concepts below have been selected for their relevance to discussions about *Birdsong*. It will aid argument and expression to become familiar with them and to use them in your discussion essays.

belle époque	French for 'beautiful era', a period lasting roughly from the end of the Franco-Prussian War (1871) to the outbreak of the First World War (1914); it was a time characterised by relative political stability between nations and a flourishing of high culture
caricature	exaggerated and ridiculous portrayal of a person built around a specific physical or personality trait, e.g. teeth, greed
cliché	predictable and overused expression or situation
colloquial	informal language of conversational speech
connotations	associations evoked by a word, e.g. 'flat' suggests dull and uninteresting; birds have negative connotations in the novel, but birdsong is associated with hope

contextuality	historical, social and cultural background of a text
criticism	evaluation of a literary text or other artistic work
defamiliarisation	making readers perceive something freshly by using devices that draw attention to themselves or by deviating from ordinary language and conventions, e.g. the passages set in the Battle of the Somme defamiliarise behaviour to raise our awareness of the soldiers' desperate situation
dialect	variety of a language used in a particular area, distinguished by features of grammar and/or vocabulary
dialogue	direct speech of characters engaged in conversation
diction	choice of words; vocabulary from a particular semantic field, e.g. religion
dramatic irony	when the audience knows something the character speaking does not, which creates humour or tension
elegy	lament for the death or permanent loss of someone or something
empathy	identifying with a character in a literary work
epiphany	sudden and striking revelation of the essence of something sublime
epitaph	words engraved upon a tombstone
figurative	using imagery; non-literal use of language
framing	a story in which another story is presented, for parallel or contrast; *Birdsong* is a framed narrative: Stephen's story is discovered and revealed by Elizabeth
Freudian	reference to the belief of the Austrian psychoanalyst that early childhood experience affects all adult responses to life through the workings of the subconscious, where repressed urges lurk and reveal themselves in dreams
genre	type or form of writing with identifiable characteristics, e.g. fairy tale
idiolect	style of speech particular to an individual character and recognisable as such

imagery	descriptive language appealing to the senses; imagery may be sustained or recur throughout texts, usually in the form of simile or metaphor
irony	language intended to mean the opposite of the words expressed; or amusing or cruel reversal of an outcome expected, intended or deserved; situation in which one is mocked by fate or the facts
juxtaposition	placing side by side for (ironic) contrast of interpretation
metaphor	suppressed comparison implied not stated, e.g. 'the wind roared'
Modernism	an artistic movement that rejected previously accepted forms of expression; it developed out of the First World War
motif	recurring verbal or structural device that reminds the audience of a theme
narrative	connected and usually chronological series of events that form a story
pastiche	literary composition made up of fragments of different styles
persona	created voice within a text who plays the role of narrator/speaker
plot	cause-and-effect sequence of events caused by characters' actions
postmodernism	contemporary literary movement, beginning around 1950
stereotype	a category of person with typical characteristics, often used for mockery
style	selection and organisation of language elements, related to genre or individual user of language
symbol	object, person or event that represents something more than itself
synopsis	summary of plot
theme	abstract idea or issue explored in a text
tone	emotional aspect of the voice of a text, e.g. 'bitter', 'exuberant'

Questions & Answers

LITERATURE

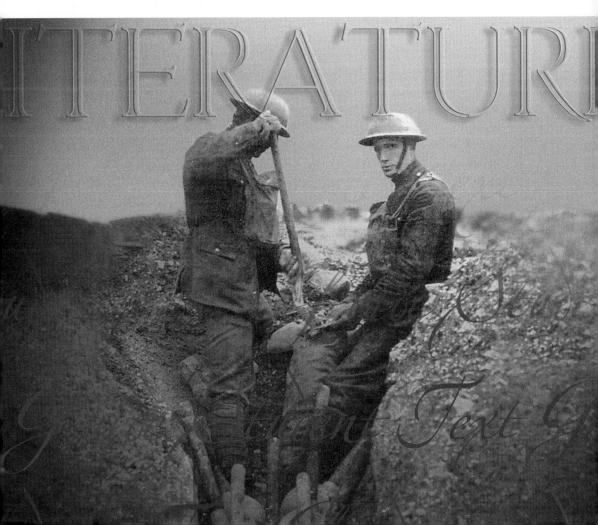

Essay questions and specimen plans

Exam essays

You may be studying *Birdsong* for an examination, or for coursework, but in both cases you need to know exactly which Assessment Objectives are being tested by your exam board and where the heaviest weighting falls. Close reference to text is required even in closed-text exams, and as quotation demonstrates 'use of text' it is often the most concise way of supporting a point. Essay questions fall into the following categories: close section analysis and relation to whole text; characterisation; setting and atmosphere; structure and effectiveness; genre; language and style; themes and issues. With the introduction of the new specifications from 2008 there is also a 'creative/transformational' option available in the AQA A specification. Remember, however, that themes are relevant to all essays and that analysis, not just description, is always required in questions that do not have an explicitly creative focus.

Exam essays should be clearly structured, briskly argued, concisely expressed, closely focused and supported by brief but constant textual references. They should show a combination of familiarity, understanding, analytical skill and informed personal response. Length is not in itself an issue — quality matters rather than quantity — but you have to prove your knowledge and fulfil the assessment criteria, and without sufficient coverage and exploration of the title you cannot be awarded a top mark. Aim realistically for approximately 12 paragraphs or four sides of A4.

Don't take up one absolute position and argue only one interpretation. There are no 'yes' or 'no' answers in literature. The other side must have something to be said for it or the question would not have been set, so consider both views before deciding which one to argue and mention the other one first to prove your awareness of different reader opinions and audience reactions. It is permissible to say your response is equally balanced, provided that you have explained the contradictory evidence and have proved that ambivalence is built into the text.

Exam essay process

The secret of exam essay success is a good plan, which gives coverage and exploration of the title and refers to the four elements of text: plot, characterisation, language and themes. Think about the issues freshly rather than attempting to regurgitate your own or someone else's ideas, and avoid giving the impression of a pre-packaged essay you are determined to deliver whatever the title.

Check your plan to see that you have dealt with all parts of the question, have used examples of the four elements of text in your support, and have analysed, not just described. Remind yourself of the Assessment Objectives (printed on the exam paper). Group points and organise the plan into a structure with numbers, brackets or arrows.

Tick off the points in your plan as you use them in the writing of your essay and put a diagonal line through the whole plan once you have finished. You can add extra material as you write, as long as it does not take you away from the outline you have constructed.

Concentrate on expressing yourself clearly as you write your essay, and on writing accurately, concisely and precisely. Integrate short quotations throughout the essay.

Allow five minutes at the end for checking and improving your essay in content and style. Insertions and crossings-out, if legible, are encouraged. As well as checking accuracy of spelling, grammar and punctuation, watch out for errors of fact, name or title slips, repetition, and absence of linkage between paragraphs. Make sure your conclusion sounds conclusive, and not as though you've run out of time, ink or ideas. A few minutes spent checking can make the difference of a grade.

Creative/transformational coursework

Think carefully about the 'angle' you wish to take with this piece of writing: it must be strong and original enough to sustain a piece of writing for approximately 1,000 words, and it must be original enough to interest the examiner and convince him or her that this is a valid interpretation of the text.

What is important is that you try to capture the 'voice' of the writer or narrator: this means that you write in a style that is sympathetic to the writer's aims and intentions and does not become a parody or a caricature.

Planning practice

It is a useful class activity to play at being examiners and to set essay titles in groups and exchange them for planning practice. This makes you think about the main issues — some perhaps not previously considered — and which episodes would lend themselves as support for whole-text questions. Try to get into the way of thinking like an examiner and using their kind of language for expressing titles, which must avoid vagueness and ambiguity.

Using some of the titles below, practise planning essay titles within a time limit of eight minutes, using about half a page. Aim for at least ten points and know how you would support them. Use numbers to structure the plan. Get used to using note form and abbreviations for names to save time, and to either not using your text (for closed-book examinations) or using it as little as possible.

Since beginnings are the most daunting part of an essay for many students, you could also practise opening paragraphs for your planned essays. Remember to define the terms of the title, especially any abstract words, and this will give your essay breadth, depth and structure, e.g. if the word 'wartime' appears, say exactly what you take 'wartime' to mean and how it applies to the novel you have studied.

Students also find conclusions difficult so experiment with final paragraphs for the essays you have planned. The whole essay is working towards the conclusion, so you need to know what it is going to be before you start writing the essay and to make it clear that you have proved your case.

Exam questions

General questions

1 **Write about the importance of places in the telling of the narratives in three texts you have studied.**

2 **Write about the ways that writers aim to make the beginnings of their texts exciting. Refer to three texts you have studied.**

3 **Write about the importance of time in the telling of the narratives in three texts you have studied.**

4 **Write about the ways that writers explore conflict in three texts you have studied.**

5 **Write about the ways that writers present relationships in three texts you have studied.**

Passage-based questions

1 **a** Write about how Faulks tells the story in the first section of Part Five (pp. 393–98 Vintage Edition).

   b How far do you agree with the view that 'what is important about *Birdsong* is the way Faulks places his story in history'?

2 **a** Write about how Faulks introduces the story in the first section of Part One (pp. 3–8 Vintage Edition).

   b How far do you agree with the view that the passages before the war are more successful than those set during the war?

3 **a** Write about how Faulks introduces the modern part of the story at the beginning of Part Three (pp. 243–48 Vintage Edition).

   b How far do you agree that the sections set in modern England are an anticlimax after the passages set in wartime?

4 **a** Write about how Faulks describes the Battle of the Somme (pp. 224–29 Vintage Edition).

   b How successful do you think Faulks's presentation of conflict is in this novel?

5 a Write about how Faulks ends the novel (pp. 498–502 Vintage Edition).

   b To what extent is this a fitting end to the novel?

Text-specific questions

1 How does Faulks's structuring of *Birdsong* affect your interpretation of the novel?

2 Comment on the presentation of masculinity in *Birdsong*.

3 To what extent would you agree that 'despite the characters' failings and weaknesses, the novel asserts a sense of humankind's dignity in the struggle to find meaning in a compromised world'?

4 Would you agree that *Birdsong* is as much about peace as it is about war?

5 'All the major characters in *Birdsong* lose what they once cherished and, as a result, become the stronger for it.' To what extent would you agree with this statement?

6 The working title of *Birdsong* was 'How far can you go?' To what extent do you think this encapsulates an important aspect of the novel?

7 To what extent would you agree that Elizabeth Benson is just as imprisoned by her gender as Isabelle is? Support your points with close reference to the text.

8 Birth and rebirth are dominant themes in the novel: what do you think Faulks's purpose was in including them in a novel ostensibly concerned with war?

9 How important is class in shaping the lives of the central characters in *Birdsong*?

10 For one critic Faulks 'does try to say… something consoling: the past can be recovered, its code can be broken; it can be used to add meaning to contemporary life.' To what extent would you agree that he achieves this aim?

11 What is responsible for Stephen being able to embrace and forgive the German soldiers who rescue him at the end of the novel?

12 One critic has written that 'the present-day scenes in *Birdsong* are so lacklustre that they seem a kind of injustice'. To what extent is this true?

13 Compare and contrast the presentation of Stephen and Weir: which in your view is the most nihilistic in their view of life?

14 By careful comparison of two passages from *Birdsong*, explore the presentation of love.

15 By careful comparison of two passages from *Birdsong*, investigate the portrayal of the effects of the First World War on two different characters.

16 'All the best parts of *Birdsong* are set not so much in the trenches as beneath them.' To what extent would you agree with this statement?

Creative/transformational

1 Imagine that you are Isabelle and you have just received Stephen's letter written on the eve of the Battle of the Somme. Write a reply capturing Faulks's style and tone, and building on Faulks's realisation of the character.

2 Write an imaginary dialogue between Stephen and Elizabeth: what would they say to each other, and how would they respond to each other's thoughts? Your piece should capture Faulks's writing style.

3 Write a letter from Isabelle to Stephen just after she has left him explaining why she felt that they had to part. You should try to capture Faulks's style and tone, and build on the character of Isabelle in this piece of writing.

Specimen questions

1 a Write about how Faulks describes the Battle of the Somme (pp. 224–29 Vintage Edition).

b How successful do you think Faulks's presentation of conflict is in this novel?

Possible ideas to include in a plan

- Language: sentencing and paragraphing conveys the increasing tempo of the scene; information is given, sometimes with little supporting description. The tension grows quickly, punctuated by a knowledge of the time ('Seven-fifteen') and the inevitability of what will happen.

- Powerful imagery is used to describe the assault on the soldiers' senses: characters scream to be heard, the air is 'solid' with metal. Among all this familiar motifs can be found (such as birdsong at the bottom of p. 225).

- Faulks is showing us that this is a momentous time in history: a 'fresh world at the instant of its creation' (p. 225), characterised by isolation, brutality, mechanical death. There is a clash between the old world of Colonel Barclay ('carrying a sword', p. 226) and the new world of guns and shrapnel and barbed wire.

- The whole episode is extremely intense, and the otherworldliness of the experience is powerfully conveyed (we are struck by the men 'running up and down' the barbed wire 'in turmoil, looking for a way through', p. 227).

- This tremendous loss of British life is contrasted with the German forces' relatively light casualties: their wire is uncut, their dugouts 'intact'.

- The episode ends tragically, ironically, with Stephen having to kill one of his own men who is begging to be shot: such is the nightmare of the Somme that doing such a thing, although a crime in itself, is merciful in this context.

- The passage is one of the most successful in the novel: refer to other passages of comparable power but focus on why this is pivotal. It has great scope, sweeps across the landscape with a cinematic rush, but also never loses sight of the individuals that made up the carnage. Language, structure, movement, characterisation…all factors combine to make this a truly memorable passage, but also one that shows why the Somme was different to what had gone before, and why it marked a new, and terrible, beginning.

2 To what extent would you agree that 'despite the characters' weaknesses, the novel asserts a sense of humankind's dignity in the struggle to find meaning in a compromised world'.

Possible ideas to include in a plan

- Why did Faulks choose this double focus: what does this structure impose upon the past (and present)? It is a layered style, building on what we have experienced, but also defamiliarising the known (he challenges us to think again about what it meant to fight at this time). The use of a non-linear format and the disruption of chronological time allows Faulks to investigate over time the effects of intense feelings and emotions on the main characters. The juxtaposition of the prewar/war/modern sections are a particularly effective narrative strategy that throws into relief the horrors of the war section. The modern sections are, perhaps deliberately, and almost inevitably, less powerful than the war sections.

- Symbolism imposes 'meaning' on a meaningless world: look further at faith, rituals, superstition etc. Symbols: birdsong, birth, birds. Look also at how style reflects subject: various passages describing the Somme show the horror of war, and the language is appropriately fragmented. But there are passages that describe the dignity of loss, of beauty, and they are elegiac. Look at the beauty of the language, written to describe profound truths.

- Meaning asserts itself at the end of the novel, and it is done through Stephen: he moves from being emotionally dead, or empty, at the beginning of the war chapters to being someone desperate to live by their end: he becomes curious about life and, crucially, is prepared, in his embracing of Levi, to forgive. There is no epiphany at the novel's conclusion — the novel is too realistic for this — but there is a realisation that life and love, despite all the darkness that man can create, are able to survive. The world will always have birdsong.

Sample essays

Below are two essays of different types, both falling within the top band. You can judge them against the text's Assessment Objectives for your exam board and decide on the mark you think each deserves and why. You may be able to see ways in which each could be improved in terms of content, style and accuracy.

Sample essay 1

To what extent would you agree that 'despite the characters' failings and weaknesses, the novel asserts a sense of humankind's dignity in the struggle to find meaning in a compromised world'?

Each of the main characters in *Birdsong* appears to be searching for something that will add greater meaning to their lives. Some fail in their search and some are successful, but Faulks does not at any point ask us to think that there is any hidden pattern, or fundamental design, to our lives. These characters, we feel, are well-rounded, 'real', and the vagaries

that they endure are ones that we can sympathise with. Faulks portrays love that cannot defy or overcome circumstances: indeed, it is compromised throughout the novel. Yet it is arguable that for many of the characters, love can impose meaning on a world that would otherwise be denied it. Faulks demonstrates the idea that where love is broken down by circumstance, the characters inherit weaknesses and are thus incapable of imposing meaning on their individual compromised existences.

The changes in Stephen after Isabelle leaves him are the result of the exterior world affecting his interior self. They are not innate weaknesses that cause him to experience failings; they are the result of living in a compromised world. He changes because of Isabelle, because of his experiences with her, and finally because of the war. Stephen becomes very bitter after Isabelle leaves him; he recalls to Weir that her departure was 'as though [he] were a child and [his] mother or father had vanished'. This reference to childhood in the context of Isabelle's disappearance is deeply symbolic of Stephen's instinctive dependency. The lack of love and care that he experienced in early life and the resulting wish he has to rely on the love of another is directly projected onto Isabelle. Through Stephen's narrative we learn of the profound effect that Isabelle had on Stephen's life. Arguably, it was his experiences with Isabelle that shaped Stephen's existence and thus laid the foundations for many of his weaknesses. The loss of innocence that Stephen experiences is suggestive of the destructive nature of reality to those who were previously ignorant of it. This new-found realism is marked by a change in Stephen's demeanour, from an expressive character to a cold-hearted and emotionless man.

Some hope in the novel can be found through the characters' retention of their dignity. Faulks illustrates this concept through the thoughts of Jack Firebrace, and his realisation that 'Their failings were not innate, but were the result of where they had gone wrong, or been coarsened by experiences' is not entirely bleak as his belief that 'in their hearts they remained perfectible' implies that there is hope; that mankind can be rescued from the depths of its own failings. Faulks is suggesting that for every flaw and weakness that the characters possess, there can be redemption, that mankind can adapt, in order to find meaning and thus to remain dignified in a world that is so profoundly compromised.

Faulks wishes us to see that hope, like despair, is fundamental to the human condition. How else can we explain Stephen's frantic — and successful — attempt to stay alive after being buried with Jack? Indeed, it is Jack Firebrace who more accurately supports Georg Lukacs's statement that 'the innermost being is determined by objective forces in society'. Jack changes profoundly because of what he has experienced, and he does so in a way that we can entirely sympathise with. It is he who symbolises the victory of despair, but Faulks tempers this outwardly nihilistic attitude by dignifying his death: 'What I have seen…I'm glad.' If that statement had gone unanswered then Faulks's position would have been bleak indeed; it adds power to the counter-argument that the plea for hope is put by Stephen when he says 'There will always be hope, Jack'.

Dignity can be viewed retrospectively and this is shown in the structure of *Birdsong*. What dignity there is is often conferred on the dead by the living; the same can be said of meaning. In retrospect we might see, for example, Weir's death as an event integral to a larger design, a plan that ultimately contributed to the defeat of Germany. We can also see the war graves, in their ordered rows, the poppies pinned neatly to each lapel, the hymns and poems, the sermons and songs, as something integral to the war: but they are the living's attempt to impose meaning and order on something that continues to reject it.

The double focus of Faulks's narrative complements the structure of his novel: the reader is presented with a double focus: we witness the past in coexistence with the present. The transgression of boundaries both in genre and in time creates a sense of defamiliarisation: the juxtaposition of the prewar/war/modern sections is a particularly effective narrative strategy that throws into relief the traumas of the war sections. The modern sections are, perhaps deliberately, and almost inevitably, less powerful than the war sections. Unearthing Stephen Wraysford's experiences emphasises to Elizabeth the relative triviality of her existence, leading her to conclude that 'in her generation there was no intensity'. The solution to her emptiness is the same as Isabelle's and through her pregnancy the themes of hope, dignity and meaning are represented. The symmetry of humanity's cycle is also expressed, as her birth can be seen as a rebirth: it was 'a promise made by [her] grandfather', described as 'another chance'.

It is this note of optimism that seems to end the book. Robert's ebullience at the birth of his son is spontaneous and affirmative: he sends up a hail of conkers — symbols of childhood innocence themselves — into the branches overhead. It seems that the world has been reborn; but, crucially, the final note in the book belongs to that symbol of death and indifference — a bird — and it is this voice, 'ambiguous...grating' that resonates with us, the 'still living', the survivors of something immensely great and unshakeable. It acts as a salient, arresting image: that at the very moment of life there is a dark margin, an echo, of death. All we can do is hope that in continuing to connect with the past, with those who have gone, we can avoid their mistakes, but we cannot avoid its final call.

Sample essay 2

Remind yourself of the passage in the novel that begins on p. 239 ('It was like a resurrection...') and ends on p. 240 ('Hold on, hold on'). Analyse Faulks's language closely and consider the themes explored in this passage.

Through a combination of powerful dialogue and memorable, figurative imagery, Sebastian Faulks creates a vivid picture of psychological, physical and even linguistic trauma. Here, as in much of the novel, reality is dismantled, or reassessed, and what passes for normality is, when taken out of context, both tragic and absurd. Alienation, the loss of faith, the emptiness of conflict, death, the banality of war and evil, rebirth...all these themes, which can be found elsewhere in the novel, are here, sometimes buried, but also explicit.

The reader sees the imposition of modern ideas upon characters who, in reality, would perhaps not have understood such rarely articulated fears. In doing so, Faulks undermines all sense of order that the war may previously have represented to his main characters. He shows us unequivocally here that this is a crime against human nature, as well as against universal order. The characters themselves are not nihilists; the world in which they dwell has become nihilistic.

The First World War marked, in many ways, the beginning of the twentieth century with the largest loss of life that the human race had ever seen. Faulks explores the nature of this conflict and allows a greater understanding of the historical context of the novel through effective imagery, and thus develops key underlying themes, repeated throughout the novel. These themes are all displayed in this passage as Faulks describes the horrors of the Somme 'like a resurrection in a cemetery twelve miles long'. Here, in the opening sentence of this extract, the motif of rebirth is first introduced to the novel. It is extremely vivid, resembling, in places, the Book of Revelations.

These men lie wounded as society — the world that they knew — begins to collapse around them, and although overcome with pain and distraught from fatigue, they scream as they realise they have 'done something terrible'. Now they must be reborn into the new social order they have created as they crawl back from their near-death experiences: the soldiers clamber back to an unrecognisable reality through the damp and the mud. In fact, the earth would seemingly rather 'disgorge a generation' than take these men who have offended it so badly. This image of the earth itself vomiting adds to the overwhelming sense of disgust at the atrocious situation (it overwhelms the reader, but it also overwhelms the characters and nature within the narrative). In exaggerating the pain and horror of the men who have died or are in the process of dying, Faulks forms the basis of the 'new world' that the reader encounters later in the passage. By depicting a new world, Faulks produces a different perspective from which his characters may view these happenings, this crime against nature, thus making it almost unreal because they see it anew. As Michael and Stephen watch the 'bent, agonised shapes' looming all around them they become alienated from their own world, the earth that they know. This use of the noun 'shapes' aids the process of de-familiarisation in this passage as it becomes difficult to separate the characters (filled as they are with life) from mere objects of war.

Faulks uses the speech and actions of his characters to further develop these repeated themes and also to depict the effect that the war has on all aspects of life. Stephen speaks in a comforting, parental tone in an attempt to calm Weir down, reassuring him that everything is 'all right'. The author uses deliberately provocative, emotive language to promote in us sympathy for the main characters. As befits his status in the army, Wraysford is trying to keep control of the situation and help those of a lower rank than him (rather like a surrogate father to a child). However, while he maintains a relaxed and composed façade, as he realises what it is that has caused Weir to start 'shaking' he begins to lose his own grip on reality. His ear must become 'used to the absence of guns', he must try not to leave all sight and memory of what the world was like before the war behind, as the absence of blood now seems almost more peculiar than blood itself. Stephen slowly begins to realise in this desperate moment of chaos that 'if he did not fight to control himself, he might never return to the reality in which he had lived'. This offence against nature has created a sense of disembodiment in both a physical and a mental sense. The nightmarish living conditions are brought into context as we see the minds of both Weir and Stephen polluted by the images of war. The tragic loss of life is taking place all around them: it has become a routine occurrence. This astonishing massacre, these evil doings of man, have become reduced to something banal. Gradually, man has transformed himself into his tribal, primitive self and it is as if Weir is the only one who sees it, beckoning the rest of humanity to 'listen to it'.

As Weir cries out for help from some unearthly source the reader slowly witnesses the loss of the meaning of words; Faulks's characters begin to lose sight of the meaning of life. This last whimper for aid has universality, and in this existential moment of despair, both Stephen and Michael realise that the world no longer makes as much sense as it used to. Weir's crying and trembling reinforces the fact that not only the British but all men involved in this war have been dislocated, and this displacement begins to have an effect on his language as his words begin to signify only emptiness. As he screams 'Oh God, oh God' all Weir is successful in doing is reminding the reader, Stephen and himself of God's non-existence and hence the emptiness all around him infecting his speech. Although this expresses the loss of faith, the turn to 'God' is instinctive. It is simply a last resort for help and forgiveness as there is nothing else that he is able to do. Somewhat unfairly, men feel that they will be punished for entering or taking part in a war that they didn't understand in the first place, for doing what they were told, when the reality is that mentally, through their loss of faith or their near-death experiences, they have already been permanently scarred. Essentially the 'new world' in which Stephen and Michael reside is fraught with panic, death and chaos and thus is essentially empty of anything that these men formerly knew. The removal of what seems like all earthly moral substance is what creates this new, nihilistic world of spiritual nothingness.

Further study

There are many books about the First World War. A very good — and brief and accessible — history of the conflict is Norman Stone's *First World War: A Short History* (2008, Penguin).

There are many other resources for a student to make use of in researching the First World War. Here is a selective bibliography of texts that will aid you in understanding the complexities of the First World War:

Fiction, memoirs, poetry

Blunden, E. (1982) *Undertones of War*, Penguin.

Fitzgerald, F. S. (1955) *Tender is the Night*, Penguin.

Graves, R. (1960) *Goodbye to All That*, Penguin.

Gurney, I. (1982) *Collected Poems* (ed. P. J. Kavanagh), Oxford University Press.

Gurney, I. (1984) *War Letters* (ed. R. K. R. Thornton), Hogarth.

Hemingway, E. (1929) *A Farewell to Arms*, Penguin.

Hill, S. (1989) *Strange Meeting*, Penguin.

Jones, D. (1987) *In Parenthesis*, Faber.

Owen, W. (1963) *Collected Poems* (ed. with an introduction and notes by C. Day Lewis and a memoir by Edmund Blunden), Chatto & Windus.

Owen, W. (1967) *Collected Letters* (eds Harold Owen and John Bell), Oxford University Press.

Remarque, E. M. (1987) *All Quiet on the Western Front* (trans. A. W. Wheen), Picador.

Sassoon, S. (1945) *Siegfried's Journey 1916–1920*, Faber.

Sassoon, S. (1961) *Collected Poems 1908–1956*, Faber.

Toynbee, P. (1954) *Friends Apart*, MacGibbon & Kee.

Histories and cultural studies

Anderson, B. (1983) *Imagined Communities*, Verso.

Bergonzi, B. (1965) *Heroes' Twilight*, Constable.

Bond, B. (ed.) (1991) *The First World War and British Military History*, Oxford University Press.

Brownlow, K. (1979) *The War, the West and the Wilderness*, Secker & Warburg.

Cannadine, D. (1984) 'Death, Grief and Mourning in Modern Britain', in J. Whalley (ed.) *Mirrors of Mortality*, Europa.

Capa, R. (1985) *Photographs* (eds Richard Whelan and Cornell Capa), Faber.

Clark, A. (1991) *The Donkeys*, Pimlico.

Dyer, G. (1994) *The Missing of the Somme*, Phoenix.

Ferro, M. (1973) *The Great War*, Routledge.

Foot, M. R. D. (1990) *Art and War*, Headline.

Fussell, P. (1975) *The Great War and Modern Memory*, Oxford University Press.

Hibberd, D. (1992) *Wilfred Owen: The Last Year*, Constable.

Hynes, S. (1990) *A War Imagined: The First World War and English Culture*, Bodley Head.

Hynes, S. (1992) *The Auden Generation*, Pimlico.

Larkin, P. (1983) *Required Writing*, Faber.

Liddell Hart, B. H. (1970) *History of the First World War*, Cassell.

Macdonald, L. (1978) *They Called it Passchendaele*, Michael Joseph.

Macdonald, L. (1980) *The Roses of No Man's Land*, Michael Joseph.

Macdonald, L. (1987) *1914*, Michael Joseph.

Orwell, G. (1970) *The Collected Essays, Journalism and Letters*, Vol. 1, Penguin.

Parker, P. (1987) *The Old Lie: the Great War and the Public School Ethos*, Constable and Co.

Robbins, K. (1984) *The First World War*, Oxford University Press.

Stallworthy, J. (1974) *Wilfred Owen*, Oxford University Press.

Taylor, A. J. P. (1966) *The First World War*, Penguin.

Viney, N. (1991) *Images of Wartime*, David & Charles.

Whelan, R. (1985) *Robert Capa: A Biography*, Faber.

Winter, D. (1979) *Death's Men*, Penguin.

Young, J. E. (1993) *The Texture of Memory: Holocaust Memorials and Meaning*, Yale University Press.

Anthologies

Glover, J. and Silkin, J. (1989) *The Penguin Book of First World War Prose*, Penguin.

Macdonald, L. (1988) *1914–1918: Voices and Images from the Great War*, Michael Joseph.

Silkin, J. (ed.) (1981) *The Penguin Book of First World War Poetry* (2nd edn), Penguin.

Stallworthy, J. (1988) *The Oxford Book of War Poetry*, Oxford University Press.

Vansittart, P. (1981) *Voices from the Great War*, Cape.

Criticism

A good critical study of Faulks's novels — including *Birdsong* — is *Sebastian Faulks: The Essential Guide* (2002, Vintage Living Texts) by Margaret Reynolds and Jonathan Noakes.

Faulks has his own website (www.sebastianfaulks.com), which is a good resource for students of his work; it is also worth looking at his entry on the Contemporary Writers website: www.contemporarywriters.com/authors/?p=auth3

There are many interviews with Faulks available on the internet, and although he discusses *Birdsong* in many of them, for the most part he talks about later books, or about writing in general. Nevertheless, students of his work might be interested in visiting these sites:

www.guardian.co.uk/books/2005/aug/21/fiction.sebastianfaulks

www.guardian.co.uk/books/2008/mar/16/fiction.sebastianfaulks

www.youtube.com/watch?v=Kc-TCH_-tw4&feature=related

Other websites with information

For general reference:
www.britannica.com

en.wikipedia.org/wiki/Main_Page

For resources specific to the war:
The BBC's site is extremely good and user-friendly:
www.bbc.co.uk/history/worldwars/wwone

www.nationalarchives.gov.uk/pathways/firstworldwar/index.htm

info.ox.ac.uk/jtap

net.lib.byu.edu/english/WWI/toc/toc.html

www.ww1photos.com

www.firstworldwar.com

www.iwm.org.uk

Film version

Although the film of *Birdsong* has not been produced at the time of going to press, ten years after rights were purchased, it is allegedly being made by Working Title for release in 2009.